Readers love
ANDREW GREY

Fire and Agate

"Andrew Grey did it again with a wonderful plot and complex characters."

—OptimuMM

Heart Untouched

"*Heart Untouched* is a sweet romance with… a nice pace, with low angst and a lovely happy ending."

—Gay Book Reviews

"It's full of honest emotions, well-laid plans, and very romantic – especially the ending!"

—Rainbow Book Reviews

All for You

"…Andrew Grey always comes up with something new and enlightening."

—Paranormal Romance Guild

"In Andrew Grey style, he delivers another well-written, easy read, with drama, danger, humor and a heartwarming relationship."

—The Novel Approach

More praise for
ANDREW GREY

Running to You

"As always Andrew has outdone himself with this story. I urge you to go out and get your copy so you can get lost in Carlos and Billy Joe's world."

—Love Bytes

"Andrew Grey always manages to pull at my heartstrings in so many ways. This book is no exception…"

—Diverse Reader

Smoldering Flame

"Andrew Grey did such an amazing job on this book. It is truly an emotional read."

—Gay Book Reviews

"This is a beautiful story…"

—Paranormal Romance Guild

Buried Passions

"The story blends in interesting themes of prejudice, and not just homophobia. The anti-immigrant sentiment was dealt with in a realistic way. And the Big City versus small town mentality was handled well, too."

—Joyfully Jay

"…this is a well written low angst love story."

—Open Skye Book Reviews

By ANDREW GREY

Accompanied by a Waltz
All for You
Between Loathing and Love
Borrowed Heart
Buried Passions
Chasing the Dream
Crossing Divides
Dominant Chord
Dutch Treat
Eastern Cowboy
In Search of a Story
New Tricks
Noble Intentions
North to the Future
One Good Deed
The Playmaker
Rebound
Reunited
Running to You
Saving Faithless Creek
Shared Revelations
Three Fates
To Have, Hold, and Let Go
Turning the Page
Unfamiliar Waters
Whipped Cream

ART
Legal Artistry • Artistic Appeal
Artistic Pursuits • Legal Tender

BOTTLED UP
The Best Revenge • Bottled Up
Uncorked • An Unexpected Vintage

BRONCO'S BOYS
Inside Out • Upside Down
Backward • Round and Round

THE BULLRIDERS
A Wild Ride • A Daring Ride
A Courageous Ride

BY FIRE
Redemption by Fire
Strengthened by Fire
Burnished by Fire • Heat Under Fire

CARLISLE COPS
Fire and Water • Fire and Ice
Fire and Rain
Fire and Snow • Fire and Hail
Fire and Fog

CARLISLE DEPUTIES
Fire and Flint • Fire and Granite
Fire and Agate

CHEMISTRY
Organic Chemistry • Biochemistry
Electrochemistry
Chemistry Anthology

DREAMSPUN DESIRES
#4 – The Lone Rancher
#28 – Poppy's Secret
#60 – The Best Worst Honeymoon Ever

EYES OF LOVE
Eyes Only for Me • Eyes Only for You

FOREVER YOURS
Can't Live Without You
Never Let You Go

GOOD FIGHT
The Good Fight • The Fight Within
The Fight for Identity
Takoda and Horse

Published by DREAMSPINNER PRESS
www.dreamspinnerpress.com

By ANDREW GREY

HEARTS ENTWINED
Heart Unseen • Heart Unheard
Heart Untouched

HOLIDAY STORIES
Copping a Sweetest Day Feel • Cruise
for Christmas
A Lion in Tails • Mariah the Christmas
Moose
A Present in Swaddling Clothes
Simple Gifts
Snowbound in Nowhere • Stardust

LAS VEGAS ESCORTS
The Price • The Gift

LOVE MEANS…
Love Means… No Shame
Love Means… Courage
Love Means… No Boundaries
Love Means… Freedom
Love Means … No Fear
Love Means… Healing
Love Means… Family
Love Means… Renewal
Love Means… No Limits
Love Means… Patience
Love Means… Endurance

LOVE'S CHARTER
Setting the Hook • Ebb and Flow

PLANTING DREAMS
Planting His Dream
Growing His Dream

REKINDLED FLAME
Rekindled Flame • Cleansing Flame
Smoldering Flame

SENSES
Love Comes Silently
Love Comes in Darkness
Love Comes Home
Love Comes Around
Love Comes Unheard
Love Comes to Light

SEVEN DAYS
Seven Days • Unconditional Love

STORIES FROM THE RANGE
A Shared Range • A Troubled Range
An Unsettled Range
A Foreign Range • An Isolated Range
A Volatile Range • A Chaotic Range

STRANDED
Stranded • Taken

TALES FROM KANSAS
Dumped in Oz • Stuck in Oz
Trapped in Oz

TALES FROM ST. GILES
Taming the Beast
Redeeming the Stepbrother

TASTE OF LOVE
A Taste of Love • A Serving of Love
A Helping of Love • A Slice of Love

WITHOUT BORDERS
A Heart Without Borders
A Spirit Without Borders

WORK OUT
Spot Me • Pump Me Up
Core Training
Crunch Time • Positive Resistance
Personal Training
Cardio Conditioning
Work Me Out Anthology

Published by DREAMSPINNER PRESS
www.dreamspinnerpress.com

REBOUND

ANDREW GREY

Published by

DREAMSPINNER PRESS

5032 Capital Circle SW, Suite 2, PMB# 279, Tallahassee, FL 32305-7886 USA
www.dreamspinnerpress.com

Rebound
© 2019 Andrew Grey.

Cover Art
© 2019 Kanaxa.
Cover content is for illustrative purposes only and any person depicted on the cover is a
model.

Trade Paperback ISBN: 978-1-64405-148-1
Digital ISBN: 978-1-64405-141-2
Library of Congress Control Number: 2018960695
Trade Paperback published February 2019
v. 1.0

Printed in the United States of America

This paper meets the requirements of
ANSI/NISO Z39.48-1992 (Permanence of Paper).

For my mom,
who passed away when I was in the middle of writing this story.
And to Lynn, who helped me through to the other side.

CHAPTER 1

"DON'T YOU dare say it," Bri said with a scowl that threatened to spear the team trainer right through the heart. "I can see you getting ready to use that tone with me, and only my mother calls me by my full name... ever."

"Well, being a total stubborn jackass is not going to help your knee heal or get you back on the court," Jack said with an equal dose of bullheadedness. "I know you're impatient, but cut it out. You can be aggressive on the court, but here, it's only going to hurt you. And you know damned well I'm not going to let you play until you have full extension. Otherwise, you're going to injure it again, and then you'll be right back in the same place, only this time with a double injury. And you know what the team will do then." He drew his finger across his throat in dramatic fashion.

Bri stifled a cringe. Being cut from the Philadelphia Rockets—his dream NBA team—was the last thing he wanted. Lately he'd been giving a lot of thought to what he would do when his playing days were over. And the truth was, he had no idea. That frightened the absolute fuck out of him, enough that he felt like throwing up all over Jack's shoes. "I know."

Jack thumped him on the shoulder. "You're getting older. It happens to all of us, but it's not all bad. You're the team leader and they need your experience. But things are taking longer to heal now, and you have to do what the therapists tell you." Jack made it sound so reasonable.... But Bri wasn't afraid of hard work—hell, he excelled at it. Only, the therapists he'd seen had all seemed afraid to push him. So he'd had to do it himself.

"I try. But they don't seem to understand that I need to get back up to playing condition as soon as possible." He actually growled at

Jack, who rolled his eyes. Jack Harker had been around long enough that it just rolled off his back. "What am I going to do?"

Jack blew air out of his mouth as he thought. "You've been through the therapists that the team uses, and none of them want to see you again." Jack pulled open the drawer of his desk. "I have notes from all of them asking that I not send you their way again." Jack's lips didn't curl upward at all. "They describe you as grumpy, bossy, unruly, and impossible to work with." He let the pages drop to the polished surface of the desk. "I don't know what to do with you. I really don't."

Bri blinked, suddenly a little light-headed. "Is that true?"

"Yes. You yelled at one of the therapists so loudly that the other patients complained. No one else in that office is going to take you on either." Jack sighed. "You need to understand that you have to work with therapists, not against them. They can't help you if you won't help yourself."

Bri took a deep breath, then released it. "Okay. But none of them seemed to understand how important this is. It's my life!"

Jack stood, leaning over the desk. "What you don't understand is that working with you is not the end-all, be-all of their existence. You are a patient, a client they work with, not the most important thing in their lives. These are people with families and friends, and they don't need ulcers because they're trying to help you. Got it?" Jack's eyes blazed in a way Bri had never seen before.

"I got it." Man, he hadn't realized that he'd taken his frustration out on the others. Shit, he wasn't a dick, not really. "Where do we go from here?" He'd come into this meeting ready to fight, and now it was gone out of him. His knee still ached on a daily basis, and using crutches sucked the big one.

Jack sat down and leaned back as though he were thinking, but Bri knew this was the crux of their entire conversation and that Jack had been leading him here the entire time. "We need to find you a new therapist, and you have to do what he says. You will follow the program he lays out for you and stick to it. The season starts in three months, which means you have to be in top shape well before that. Two months is what you have, so you need to make the most of it."

"I will. But who is my therapist?" Bri asked.

Jack got this cockeyed, almost cruel smile. "I don't know. I don't have one. Word has gotten around." He put his hands behind his head. "I made a few calls and got nowhere. So, this one is up to you. Try the Yellow Pages." He grinned. "Seriously."

His phone rang. Jack raised a finger to Bri, silently asking him to hold on to that thought, then snatched it up. "This is Jack. ... Awesome, thanks for returning my call. I have a bit of a problem. ... Yes, you heard right." Jack met his gaze, and Bri knew he was the subject of the conversation. Bri grew more nervous by the second as Jack hummed and agreed with whoever was on the line. "You're a prince, you know that?" Jack began writing on a slip of paper. "Thanks so much. Give my best to Monty and maybe we can get together soon." Jack smiled and hung up. He turned to Bri. "You, my friend, are one lucky son of a bitch."

Bri glowered a little, narrowing his eyes. "Okay, how?"

"I put some feelers out because we were running out of ideas. You remember Hunter Davis? He was injured at the end of the last football season. I called him to find out who he used for his rehab, and he gave me the name." Jack didn't pass the sheet of paper over.

"Good." He reached out for it, but Jack didn't move.

"You know Hunter, right?" Jack asked.

"I play poker with him a few times a month." He started to roll his eyes and stopped himself. Jack was trying to help, and he needed to stop acting like a dick. "Yeah, I know him. He's a stand-up guy."

"And even he's heard about you. Like I said, word gets around. So expect some shit about it at your next game." Jack passed the scrap of paper across the desk. "This is the guy that Hunter used, and he says he was incredible. He's also a friend of his husband Monty's, so if you piss this therapist off, it's likely you aren't going to be invited to any more poker nights." Jack glared at him hard, and Bri nodded. Monty was a great guy, and no one wanted to be uninvited to poker night.

3

"I understand." He was tired of his knee hurting, of having to wear a brace and use crutches. Why couldn't anyone understand that all he wanted was to be himself again? Was that so much to ask? "I'll call him first thing and make an appointment."

"Good." Jack leaned forward. "And whatever you do, be nice to the guy. Maybe treat him like a friend instead of a servant. After all, he is the friend of a friend." Jack waved him out of the office as his phone rang again. "And for God's sake, do what he says and follow his regimen. Give your torn ligaments a chance to heal properly and don't overdo it." Then he turned away to answer the phone. Bri got his crutches from where he'd leaned them against the chair, shifting them under his arms and getting up, hobbling his way out of the office.

He smiled at Janet, the team receptionist, stopping to talk with her for a few minutes before continuing out of the arena office and down to his car.

He lowered himself into the driver's seat with a sigh and got himself inside. It was a good thing he'd hurt his left leg or he wouldn't have been able to drive, and that would've been total crap. As it was, his mother was hinting that she should come stay with him. Bri loved his mother—she was a force to be reckoned with, in a really good way. His father was the educated one in the family, but his mother was the one who ran things and brought everyone together. Bri's big sister had gone on to medical school, and his older brother was an elementary school principal in Carlisle, a small Pennsylvania town west of Harrisburg. Bri loved his mom, but at a distance, definitely a distance. She was someone who liked things done her own way.

Taking a breather, he pulled out his phone and called his new therapist. He might as well get this over with. The phone rang and rang, and Bri figured he was going to have to leave a message. Then suddenly, someone picked up.

"Hello, OK Physical Therapy, Obie speaking. How can I help you?" a breathless man answered. At least Bri thought it was a man. It was a little difficult to tell.

"I'm Bri Early, from the Philadelphia Rockets. I was told that you can help me." He kept his voice as calm as he could make it, even though his belly was doing flips. If he didn't heal and regain his strength, he was going to be cut from the team. Contract or not, his career would be over. And that was something he didn't want to contemplate.

"Yes. Monty said he was passing on my contact information." He still sounded a little out of breath.

"I don't mean to be pushy, but...."

The guy laughed. "You're talking pushy with a physical therapist? That's a good one. I can out-pushy anyone." He continued chuckling. "Let me guess, you want an appointment as soon as possible so we can meet and get started." The guy talked a mile a minute. "You're in luck, because I had a cancellation, so I can see you for an evaluation in two hours if you're available. Then we can put together a plan to get you on your feet and back on the court. Does that work?" A beeping sounded in the background behind him. "Fiddlesticks."

"Is something wrong?"

"No. I overcooked my lunch." He giggled this time, and Bri wondered just what he was letting himself in for. "So, will I see you this afternoon?"

"Yes." At least he could get in right away.

"Sounds good." He rattled off the address, and Bri had to work quickly to get it into his phone. Then he read it back. "What sort of office do you have?"

"I don't work in an office. I have a private practice and I work out of the back of my home. I don't talk about other clients and I keep everything confidential. I have a number of high-profile clients who use my services because no one sees them coming and going. The house has an alley in back, with a parking space under the carport that you can use. Then come right through the gate and up to the office door."

"All right." At least there weren't going to be other people around to stare at him, like at the first place he tried. It was supposed to have been exclusive too, but that's sure not the way he remembered it. He shook his head, trying to forget the embarrassing episode.

"Do you have any other questions?"

"What sort of records should I bring?"

"If you have your latest X-rays, that would help. Today, we'll do an evaluation and I'll try to make you as comfortable as I possibly can. Then I'll check the condition of your muscles and we'll go from there. Please call me if you have any questions, and I'll see you at two."

Bri ended the call and put the address in his GPS so he'd know where he was going. It turned out one of his favorite restaurants was on the way, so he decided to stop there for lunch. Since he'd been hurt, he'd been careful to watch what he ate, and a Middle Eastern vegetarian lunch sounded really good. Bri turned the car engine on and pulled out of his space.

A LITTLE before his appointed time, he pulled into the carport as instructed and got out, entering the yard through the back gate. It took him a few seconds to close it behind him, but once he turned around, it was as if he had stepped into another world. The small yard was stunning, with running water, a bridge, and flowers and plants everywhere—a calming, quiet Eden.

"Mr. Early?" a small man asked as he stepped out the back door of the house. He was fashionably thin, with bright, Easter egg–yellow short hair. "Come on through. My last client just left a few minutes ago."

"This is gorgeous back here," he commented as he used his crutches to navigate the paver stone pathway, trying not to stare at the man's bright hair color, but failing. Paths led off in different directions, presumably to different areas of the garden.

"Be careful." His new therapist hurried over, lifting something off the path. "Don't want to hurt George."

"A turtle?" Bri asked, coming to a stop as the box turtle headed for cover. "You have a turtle."

"Two of them. That was George. Gracie is hiding somewhere." He smiled. "She comes out in the evening. They love strawberries, so I keep some on hand for them." He turned, leading the way inside, holding the door for Bri and then closing it behind him.

The back room of the house was a large single room, fitted with therapy equipment, a massage table, and almost everything the larger clinics had, except this was quiet and more intimate, with soft music piped in.

"I'm Obie. It's good to meet you." He held out his hand, and Bri shifted the crutches under his arm, then took it.

"It's good to meet you." He hobbled over to the nearest chair and sat down.

Obie drew one over and sat across from him. "I know what happened to you. I saw a replay on YouTube. After you called, I brought up the videos. The source of an injury is often a good indicator of where to begin treatment and rehabilitation. You tore your ligaments and meniscus pretty badly."

"Yes." He lifted his gaze and met the brightest, most limpid round blue eyes above gently freckled cheeks he could have possibly imagined. They had to be dinner-plate-size and seemed filled with gentle caring. It was intriguing to say the least.

"The other player should have been ejected from the game and probably the sport. The refs that night were totally blind." Obie leaned forward. "Did you bring shorts to change into? If not, I have a pair you can borrow." Bri hadn't thought about bringing anything, so Obie got up and returned with a pair of blue shorts, handing them to him, then pointing to a small room. "Go on in there and change, then we'll get started."

"Don't you have a million questions for me? The other therapists asked a barrage of questions before they began." He hopped to the changing room door.

"I'll have plenty, but I want to talk while we work." Obie closed the door, and Bri took his time getting out of his pants and into the shorts. Everything seemed to take such a long time with the crutches and the brace. He nearly fell as he pulled on the shorts, but managed to get them on, and returned to the outer room, where Obie waited for him.

"The initial injury was in an exhibition game a month ago, correct?" Obie asked. "And I'm guessing you've overdone it a couple times, and that has set back healing. Well, that isn't going to happen again. Right?"

"Yes. I want to get back to normal as quickly as possible," Bri countered.

"We all want that." Obie patted the top of the massage table. "You and I are partners now. That's how it works here. I don't have a revolving door of clients, and I get invested in your recovery." Bri sat on the edge of the table. "The team trainer sent me some basic information, but I need you to fill out these forms for me, sign them at the bottom, and then we can get started."

Obie handed him a clipboard, and Bri began filling out the paperwork. He'd done this sort of thing a million times lately, and it took just a few moments. Obie looked it over and skipped to the health questionnaire. "You aren't allergic to anything and have no other issues. That's good."

"Except I'm getting older," Bri added.

Obie *pff*ed and had him lie on his back on the table. "Come on. You can continue to do what you love as long as you want to. Look at Cher. She's still performing and singing in her seventies. And the lady looks good."

"Better living through surgery?" Bri quipped.

"Have you ever seen how active she is at one of those shows? I saw her once when I was younger." Obie gently ran his hand up Bri's leg, avoiding the knee but loosening up the other muscles.

"God, that's good," Bri groaned.

"Since your knee has been out of commission, the other muscles have taken up the slack. Even holding your leg up off the ground requires work, and those muscles need to relax as well." He continued working away. "So why are you here with me?"

Bri groaned as Obie hit a tender spot and then the muscle released. "Because I pissed off every other therapist on the planet." He closed his eyes and floated for a second. "I wanted to get better and back into playing form as fast as possible, I guess."

"Too fast," Obie said, as he continued massaging the muscles in Bri's leg. "The body needs time to heal, and what you did requires just that. See, you have cartilage and muscle, and you injured both of them. You had the surgery to deal with the meniscal tear. Now we have to let the ligaments knit together before we can work with the muscle. Otherwise we can hurt you worse."

"I get that. This isn't my first injury," Bri said without heat.

"What did the doctor say at your last examination?"

"That I need to give it time. But the longer I can't move my leg, the more muscle I'm going to lose and the harder it will be to come back. When I was twenty-two, this would have been nothing."

Obie switched his attention to the other leg. "You aren't twenty-two any longer, so the healing process requires more work." He got the muscles loose, and Bri groaned under his breath as the tension in his quads and calves released as though they were on a spring. "I believe in whole-body healing. Not just the part that's injured."

"Okay." Bri kept his eyes closed, listening to the soothing sound of Obie's voice. It had a gentling quality. He spoke just softly enough that Bri had to listen carefully, which kept his attention off his leg, especially when Obie turned his attention to his knee.

"Don't tense up. I'm not going to hurt you." He kept his touch light, and soon Bri found himself relaxing once again. "So, as I was saying. You need to eat for recovery. Plenty of protein, but make it lean, chicken and fish, plus lots of vegetables and fruit. Give your body what it wants and don't be hard on it." He continued working gently. "And no heavy drinking. The body wastes energy getting that out of your system."

"So, no onion rings, then?" Bri teased with a smile.

"Oh. Those you can have all you want, especially the ones from Blooms around the corner." Damn, Obie was teasing him back. That was unexpected. "My God, those things are my one weakness. They make them fresh, with a tempura batter that they put a little pepper in, so it has a kick. Then they serve them with ranch dressing." Obie chuckled. "I don't think that's what you were getting at, though, right? But it made me hungry."

"You?" Bri did his best to sound affronted. "Now I'm starving, and the hummus and baba ghanoush I had for lunch just isn't cutting it."

9

"From Mediterranean Garden? I love it there. They make everything fresh that morning, and you can tell by the way it tastes. Yeah, you can go there all you like."

Obie giggled, and Bri slipped his eyes open to watch him. Obie was smaller, with fewer angles and more soft lines than the guys he was usually attracted to, but he was stunning. Bri mentally shook himself. He was not going to have those kinds of thoughts. Not here.

"You're an athlete, so you know all about eating well. Be good to your body and don't strain the rest of it."

"Okay." Bri let go of his curiosity and let Obie work.

"See, we only have so much juice," he continued. "So if you strain your arm, your body has to heal both the knee and your arm. But we want all the good energy focused on your knee." He pulled his hands away, and Bri sat up slowly. Obie handed him a small bottle of water. "Drink up. You need to flush some of the toxins I just released out of your system." Obie stood close enough to him that his own fresh, clean scent filtered in over the lotion. Bri leaned in slightly, inhaling slowly just to get a little more. He stopped himself a second later, pushing the thought away. That was not what he came here for at all. Yeah, he was friends with Hunter and understood about the whole gay thing. But that wasn't for him. He couldn't risk his career that way. Bri had long ago accepted that he wasn't going to get married. He was a bachelor, he was happy, and he'd stay that way. When he needed an itch scratched, he did so discreetly and always out of town—far out of town. Damn it all, he was not letting his mind go there.

Bri pulled the top off the water bottle and drained the contents. "Is that it?" Bri got his head back where it belonged and away from the interest that certain body parts were beginning to show.

"No. Now that I have the muscles warmed up and supple, let's see where you're at. We aren't going to work too hard today. I'm going to have you lie down and we're going to check your range of motion. No quick movements and no untoward pressure." Obie helped him get settled on the table once again, and Bri slowly lifted his leg. Obie helped maneuver it, bending the knee slightly back and forth. His hands were soft, and true to his word, each movement was fluid. Their eyes kept meeting, and Bri told himself that it was because Obie was doing his job, that he was looking back at him because it was what he should do. Still, Bri couldn't seem to take his eyes off him, and he had to admit, it wasn't all because of what Obie was doing, but more about his biggest, bluest, "get lost in them and never come out again" eyes. "Can you do a little more?" Obie asked.

Bri closed his eyes, gritted his teeth, and bent his knee a fraction farther, to the point of pain. "How is that?"

"Good. Hold still." Obie measured quickly and then slowly settled his leg back on the table. "It's better than I thought it would be. You're moving your knee about 20 percent. That's not a bad starting place. We'll keep working on it as healing progresses. Okay. I'm going to give you some exercises that I want you to do at home every day. These will help keep your leg limber and the muscles supple." He took Bri through each one and had him repeat them. "Good. And don't overdo it. I usually have to scold my patients into doing their exercises, but I have a feeling that won't be the issue here."

"Probably not. I'll do them every day." Bri got up and carefully got off the table, returning to the changing room to dress in his street clothes.

"Just leave the shorts in the hamper and I'll wash them," Obie called through the door. Once again, it took him more time than he would have liked to dress and then get his brace back on. He hated the thing, but felt better once it was in place. "Put some heat on your knee if it's sore, but that shouldn't last too long. Try not to take pain medication. It dulls the body."

"Don't like pills anyway." That was the truth. "In college, the trainer…." God, he so didn't want to go there. "I stay away from as much of it as I possibly can."

"I'm aware that team trainers and doctors overprescribe sometimes and will do just about anything to keep you guys playing." He pulled up the chair and sat down again. Bri let his legs settle to the floor. It felt good to have both of them free again, for a while anyway. "I'm the same way. I'll do anything to help my clients get better. I'll work just as hard as you do. But I can't work miracles. I also advocate

11

healthy living and plenty of rest, eating right, proper, controlled exercise, and…." Obie giggled again. "I sound like a commercial, don't I? Sometimes I go on and on, I know that. Feel free to tell me to cool it. I won't get offended, I promise." He took a breath, and Bri stared at his lips a little too long, then blinked. Damn, he needed to get it together.

Obie nodded. "And drink plenty of water. Is Friday afternoon good for you?" Obie opened the laptop on the small desk. "I have two thirty open again, if that's okay." He was already typing away.

"I'll be here." Bri got his crutches and hobbled toward the door. Obie opened it, and Bri made his way back to his car, through the incredible garden. Obie followed and waited until he was back to the car, then closed the gate.

Bri got behind the wheel, sliding his crutches into the back seat and closing the door, then taking a deep breath. This was a professional relationship and nothing more. He needed to get back on his feet so he could play again. If Obie could help him do that, great. The rest of it didn't matter. He needed to keep his head in the game.

Bri started the ride home and placed a call to Jack. "I had my first appointment." He spoke through speakers built right into the car. He loved that.

"How did it go?" Jack asked.

"Pretty well, I think. He's not at all what I expected, but he seems to really know what he's doing. My leg aches a little, but it feels good too." He got on the Schuylkill Expressway and, of course, came to an almost immediate stop. Good thing he only had to go a few exits.

"I hear doubt in your voice," Jack said. "Look, you need therapy and this is the last guy available. Hang in there and get it done so we can put you back on the active roster."

"I know." He needed to put his doubts away and keep his mind on what was important—his career. Nothing else mattered. "I'll keep you posted." He ended the call, and thankfully traffic ahead began to move.

His phone rang, and Bri pressed the button on his steering wheel to answer it. "Hello."

The line crackled. "I know what you are," a mechanical voice rang through the car speakers. "And I won't allow you to taint the sport any longer. You don't seem to be able to read a message when I send it, so I'll have to try again. This time, it will hurt more than it did the last time."

"Who the hell is this?" Bri demanded, even as a chill raced up his spine. "How did you get this number?"

But nothing else came through the speakers.

CHAPTER 2

"How did it go with the client you won't talk about?" Chippy asked as he crossed his legs and sipped from his wineglass. He was seated on Obie's brand-new slimline sofa in a perfect shade of blue that matched his eyes. Or so he'd been told.

"You know I won't talk about anyone I work with, so you can stop bugging." Obie picked up his own glass and lowered himself into the perfectly offsetting chair in white. He scratched his head. "I have to wash this stuff out of my hair. I thought I'd like the yellow, but it just isn't me." He tilted his head so he could look into the mirror over the fireplace. "I think it makes me look like a lemon."

"And Lord knows you don't want to be sour," David quipped from where he sat next to Chippy. Obie had met David when he was trying to figure out the whole gay thing. Chippy had been his best friend ever since they'd been kids. The three of them were sort of the gay musketeers. "But what color will you go?" He looked aghast when Obie didn't answer. "You mean natural? How... original." He fanned himself and giggled.

"I know. I haven't gone outside with my original hair color in years, but don't worry. It's only temporary. I have to decide what I want, and this temporary stuff makes me feel kind of skanky and weird." It was supposed to wash right out, and Obie certainly hoped it did.

"After all, not everyone can have my raven locks," Chippy chimed in. Chippy had shoulder-length black hair that curled slightly and was so dark, it shone blue in the sun. Obie had always wished for hair the same color as his friend's, and had tried dying it once. His hair had turned out awful—flat, and mousy. After a few weeks, he'd buzzed his head to get rid of all of it. "So, what are we doing tonight?" Chippy asked, doing a slight hair flip. "There's a new club

14

opening downtown, and I'd like to go. It could be fun, and all the most interesting people are going to be there. Hunter Davis and Monty are supposed to be going."

"I know. Monty told me the other day. Hunter isn't too thrilled about it. But Monty wants to go, so they'll probably end up there, but not stay late."

David leaned forward. "Okay. What I want to know is if Hunter is bringing any of his football friends? I'd love to shimmy and shake up one of those guys."

"They'd break you in two," Chippy countered. "Besides, can you see those guys in a gay club? Really?"

"They're pretty cool. Monty had me over for one of Hunter's poker nights. He and I had cosmos and binged *Queer as Folk* reruns while they got all testosterone-y in the other room. They were kind of hot and pretty good guys, but I don't see any of them taking the trip to the dark side." Obie sat back, sipping from his glass.

"And he didn't invite us?" David asked, sounding dejected.

Obie rolled his eyes. "Remember the last time Monty had you two over? It was Girls Gone Wild, and you two were the girls. The squealing… and that was just Hunter when Chippy here decided he was a tree and tried to climb him." Obie glared at his friend. "Hint… humping someone's husband is not the way to get a repeat invitation."

Chippy did his best to look hurt as he probably tried to remember the evening. They'd both had way too much to drink, and Obie had ended up taking them home since he'd drawn the short straw as the designated driver. "So, you're saying the club is out?"

"What do you think? We're nobodies. So we wait in line with a hundred other people while the glitterati pass us by and we watch them go inside." Obie had had enough of that, thank you very much.

"But I love watching the glitterati, and maybe if I glitter enough, I'll get to go in." David flashed his cheeks in the light, already shining from the sparkly makeup he had on. "Come on, it will be fun. If we can't get in, then I'll buy us all munchies and we'll drown our sorrows in onion rings." He knew Obie's one weakness and was obviously willing to exploit it.

Obie set his glass on the table. "And for this little jaunt, you probably expect me to drive, right?" He'd only had about six sips of his wine, and it looked as though he wasn't going to be having any more, if history held to form. Granted, he wasn't a big drinker anyway.

"The train is only a few blocks away from here. We might be able to catch it if we got going and Miss Thing over here could do her makeup without taking three hours," Chippy teased, turning to David. "It's a great night, and we should make the most of it."

David sighed dramatically. "Fine." He stood and was already checking himself out in the mirror. "Just give me ten minutes." He rushed off and was out the front door and back within thirty seconds. Then, moving so quickly he was just a blur, he passed the doorway to the living room. Seconds later, Obie heard the thunk of the downstairs bathroom door closing.

"Ten minutes my sweet ass," Chippy said. "I bet he's in there for at least an hour." He stood. "Come on, I'll help you clear this away and then we can get going." He picked up the plates of munchies that had already been picked clean and took them to the kitchen. Obie followed with the glasses, rinsing them all out and setting them in the sink.

"I have to get some things upstairs. Be right back." Obie hurried up the stairs and into the bathroom. He pulled off his shirt, turned on the water in the tub, and stuck his head under it. The water ran yellow and he reached for shampoo, rubbing it in and scrubbing, then rinsing it out, as his unfortunate hair color ran down the drain. Then he washed it again, then a third time, until the water ran clear. Turning it off, he grabbed a towel from under the sink and dried his hair and head.

That felt damn good and his scalp felt clean. Standing up, he grabbed a comb and styled his still-wet hair a little. Then he put on his shirt and checked himself in the mirror. He looked fine, and it wasn't like he was expecting to meet the love of his life—tonight, anyway. He was going to be standing outside for hours, so what did it really matter? He glanced in the mirror, shrugged, and shook his head slightly before hanging up the towel and leaving the room.

"Are you ready?" he yelled down the stairs, grabbing his wallet and keys and sliding them in his pockets before descending the stairs.

"Wow," Chippy said as he met the others in the living room. "Is that what that stuff did to you? That orangey red color, it's…."

"My real hair," Obie said as he grabbed a dark hat, adjusting it to a jaunty angle to cover most of his hair. "Now let's get going before we miss the train." He pulled open the front door, and they stepped out into the night.

JUST AS Obie suspected, they got there only to stand in a line a block long. Worse, it hadn't moved more than ten feet in the last half hour. At this rate, they would get in next Thursday. In desperation and because he was tired of standing there, he messaged Monty and got a quick response.

I'm inside. I'll send Hunter out to get you.

The guys are with me, Obie replied.

I'll warn him. The message was followed with a happy face. And sure enough, five minutes later, Hunter, accompanied by one of the bouncers, found them and they were escorted around the rest of the line and into the club, which pulsated with energy.

"Oh my God," David said, holding on to Obie's arm as though he might faint. "Would you look at him." He pointed, and Obie let his gaze follow. "Do you think he'd let me climb him like a tree?"

"No!" Obie said firmly. "Just don't you dare." Then he turned at the sound of a familiar voice. There was his newest client, propped up on crutches.

"Hunter," he heard Bri say as they approached. "This isn't my thing. I'm happy to support the AIDS Research Council, but it's getting late. I think I'm just going to head home."

Obie was definitely surprised to see Bri here, but then, the evening was for a good cause. He liked that Bri cared enough to help out.

He was just about to go over and say something, but his friend beat him to it.

"Hi, I'm David." He held out his hand to Bri. "You're Bri Early, aren't you? I'm sure I've seen you on television. You do those luscious commercials for Chanel. I went out and bought some just because of you." He leaned closer. "Want to check it out and see?" He pressed his upturned hand forward so Bri could supposedly smell his wrist.

"Knock it off," Obie said. "Be nice. He doesn't want to smell you." He definitely needed to run a little interference.

"Yeah, none of us do," Chippy added, much to David's visible consternation. Chippy tugged David in the direction of the bar as Monty joined Hunter, wrapping an arm around him.

"Dang, half of gay Philly is here tonight." Monty looked up at Hunter, his partner. "I think I need to mark you, just so all the trolling queens will keep their damn distance," he said, louder than was necessary. The circle of guys inching their way closer seemed to back away a little, but not for long. It seemed they had their sights on Bri as well.

"I know. Thanks, Hunter, for coming to our rescue," Obie said. "I thought we'd be in that line forever."

"Speaking of rescues, do you think you could give me a little help?" Bri glanced around, his deep brown eyes a little dazed as the vultures seemed to close in.

"No problem." Obie walked to his left side, taking Bri's arm. "Let's see if we can find a table." Obie gave the onlookers his best "He's with me, bitches" look and guided his new client over to a table with a Reserved sign on it. Hunter slid right in with Monty, and Obie made sure Bri got settled before he took a place next to him.

"What can I get you?" a buff server asked, a black T-shirt, at least two sizes too small, straining over his chest and biceps.

"Club soda with lime," Bri ordered.

"I'll have the same. I need to make sure I can get my friends home in one piece." Obie thanked the server as he was leaving.

"They seem a little feral," Bri said, and Obie chuckled. Damn, he couldn't help it.

"They're good guys, believe it or not. Even if they're a little over the top sometimes." He turned to see David and Chippy on their way over, each with their hands full.

"We brought you drinks," Chippy said, putting down a cosmo in front of Monty and a beer for Hunter.

"I didn't know what you wanted," David told Bri. Then he seemed to notice how close Bri and Obie were sitting. "Hey, I saw him first." He glared at Obie.

"Stop it and get a chair." Obie wasn't going to tell them how he knew Bri; that was up to him. For now, Bri was a friend of Hunter's and that was all his friends needed to know. "This isn't a buffet where you grab the last piece of cake and guard it with your life until you get it back to the table." He rolled his eyes.

"Sure it is. This is a man buffet," Chippy said. He gestured dramatically. "Look at that guy over there." David drained his glass, then looked around, as if on the prowl and ready to hunt. Then he set his martini glass on the table and prancing-ponied away into the crowd.

"See? Feral," Bri said.

"I'm going to make sure he doesn't get punched in the face," Chippy said, then left the table as well.

"Good luck with that," Obie called over the music. He cleared his throat. If he kept this up, he was going to be hoarse by the end of the evening. "So what brings you here?" Obie asked Bri. "This doesn't look like resting and letting your knee heal." Obie got up and pulled one of the vacated chairs over for Bri to prop up his leg.

"God, that feels good."

Even though the club was packed and the sound system blaring, Obie still heard, or maybe felt, Bri's grateful sigh. "Put some heat on it when you get home," Obie said gently. "And for goodness' sake, rest it tomorrow. When I see you on Friday, we'll be working hard. I want you up for it."

"Yeah, Brighton, you need to do what the therapist says," Monty teased.

19

Bri growled. "If you're going to get loose lips, I'm taking your drink away." Bri glared at Monty, who snatched his cosmo off the table, turning to the side to protect it.

"Sorry."

"Your name is Brighton Early," Obie said with a smile.

"Yeah. I hate my name. I went by either B or Bri in school, and I beat the crap out of anyone who called me anything else. I love my mother to death—she's totally awesome—so I haven't had it changed, but dammit, can you imagine being saddled with a name like that as a kid?"

Obie smiled, and Bri growled, "Don't laugh."

"I'm not. Well, at least, not at your name. I hate my name too, though I keep it for my dad's sake," Obie explained and glanced at Monty and Hunter. "If any of you ever open your mouths about this, I will be forced to kill you, I swear." He did his best to sound threatening.

"This should be good," Monty said.

"Be nice. Obie is your friend, and remember what he did for me last year. You behave," Hunter scolded and leaned close, whispering into Monty's ear for a few seconds. Monty turned beet red. His mouth widened and his eyes grew as big as saucers. Obie knew Hunter was promising him some very naughty things.

"I'll be good, I promise," Monty said really quickly.

"Well, now that you're all sworn to secrecy, you have to pinkie swear. If you tell, I get to break your pinkies. Got it?" He glared all around the table, and they each agreed. "Okay. My entire name is Obediah Juan Kenoble." He waited, and Bri gasped.

"You're Obie Juan Kenoble? Oh... my... fucking... God!" Bri turned away, and a few seconds later, his shoulders rolled and he put his head down on the table. Obie smacked him across the back, but couldn't help laughing himself. And they weren't alone. Hunter laughed outright, and Monty had collapsed in a fit of giggles, sliding under the table and ending up on the floor.

"Come on," Hunter said as he tugged Monty back into his seat. "You're fine now." Hunter shook his head and looked at Obie. "What on earth possessed your parents to name you that?"

"Really bad luck. Obediah was my grandfather's name on my dad's side, and Dad was a huge Star Wars fan. He still sees every movie at least three times a year. I love him, so I'd never have it changed, but I go by Obie." He added with emphasis, "Remember your promises, if you want to keep your pinkies intact." He glared at Hunter and Monty before turning to Bri. "You keep my secret, and I'll keep yours."

"Deal," Bri said with a yawn. "Sorry. I'm really tired and should be going home. My therapist says I need to get plenty of rest. He's a real ballbuster, so I'd better do what he says or he'll make me pay for it." Bri winked and grabbed his crutches, just as they were suddenly blinded by an onslaught of camera flashes. Hunter and Monty leaned closer and let their pictures get taken. Bri leaned back and tried to hide behind Obie.

"Why are you here?" one of the photographers asked.

"To show support for a friend," Hunter answered easily.

"Is that why you're here, Bri?" the guy pressed, leaning forward to try to get a better picture.

"We're all here to support a good cause," Bri answered, his words a little halting. But then the club bouncers took control and led the three guys with cameras away.

"Sorry, sirs," one of the bouncers said and nodded before leaving them alone once again. Obie could tell Bri's tension had gone through the roof. His hands clenched and opened, his leg bounced slightly on the chair, and he sat as stiff as a board, the mirth of a few minutes earlier evaporating in a flash.

"I really should go." Bri got his crutches and slid out of the booth, slipping them under his arms, making his way through the crowd. Obie figured it had to be the first time in his life he had seen a man as tall as Bri's six foot six actually try to pull himself down to the point where he blended in with the crowd.

Obie met Monty's gaze, and Monty shrugged. Obie honestly hadn't given a second thought to Bri being gay during his appointment, but seeing him at the club, Obie figured it might have been a possibility. And when he'd let Obie take him by one of his huge arms.... Obie imagined fanning himself, but now he wasn't so sure what the deal was at all. Obie thought about asking Monty, but the place loud, and he wasn't going to yell across the table.

"I think I'm going to go too," Obie said. He stood and gave both Hunter and Monty a quick hug. "Would you tell my 'feral' friends where I went?" He turned to look over at the dance floor and saw Chippy making his way back with a guy on his arm. Obie waved, and Chippy nodded, blowing him a kiss. They started dancing as Obie made for the exit, catching up with Bri in the cooling evening air.

"I have two words for them. Air. Conditioning," Obie said, and Bri paused his mad, hobbling escape down the sidewalk.

"If they did, they wouldn't sell as many drinks. Places like that always keep it warmer than necessary." He paused. "Thanks for saving me in there. I really appreciate it." Bri continued walking in his stiff-backed discomfort.

"There's no need to be nervous or worried and stuff." Obie caught up with him. "I'm not going to let anything that happened tonight affect our professional relationship. I'm your therapist and you're my client. We ran into each other at a club, that's all. And it was really cool of you to come and support the charity. Even if you were a little uncomfortable."

"Well...."

"So, don't worry about anything. It's all good. I had a nice time, and I'll see you on Friday for our appointment." He half snickered, thinking of teasing Bri about his name, but stopped himself. There was no need to go there right now. But that cat was out of the bag, and it wasn't going back in.

"Okay." Bri continued a little farther before opening the door of a gorgeous black Mercedes. "How are you getting home?"

"I was going to take the train." He pointed to the subway station just up the block.

"Hop in. I'm going that way and I can drop you off." He climbed inside, putting his crutches in the back, while Obie slid into the passenger seat. He hadn't been expecting this, but decided to enjoy it as he settled into the lap of luxury and Bri navigated them out of the city.

"I had forgotten about the club opening this afternoon until Hunter called to remind me." He winced, and Obie could tell Bri's leg was probably hurting. The deep lines around his mouth were a telltale sign.

Thankfully the traffic through town was light at this hour and Bri was able to get him home relatively quickly. "Thanks so much for the ride. I really appreciate it." Obie opened the door and got out. "Be sure to put some heat on your knee when you get home. It will help."

"I'm fine," Bri said automatically.

"No, you're not. You overdid it today and you knee is aching. It's written all over your face. I know you're a big, strong athlete, but you need to take care of that leg or it isn't going to get better. Use some heat, elevate the leg, and get yourself some sleep." He patted Bri's shoulder. "God, what are you made of—rocks?" His arms were like granite. "Sorry. Get some rest and I'll see you Friday." He got out of the car and went inside as Bri pulled away.

Obie stopped at the front door, thinking. Bri had been mortified when those guys with cameras had tried to take his picture. And the way he'd sat in stony silence the entire ride? Obie unlocked the door and mentally drew a line through Bri's Friday therapy appointment. The guy was probably going to cancel. He had a sense about these things.

CHAPTER 3

BRI WOULD have been pacing the floor if he hadn't been on crutches. He checked the time again and sighed. He had to leave now if he was going to make it on time. He'd picked up the phone to cancel more than once, but hadn't done it. After he'd rested his knee, it felt better and the muscles had actually relaxed. "Man up," he told himself as he got his keys and left the kitchen, heading into the garage. He'd never been one to shy away from hard work or the tough things in life, and he hadn't gotten where he was by resting on his laurels and hoping that things would work out. It also didn't help that Jack had called him last night to remind him of the importance of getting back into playing form. So off he went to his therapy appointment.

Twenty minutes later, hobbling into Obie's garden, he took a deep breath as wild ginger and maybe even jasmine wrapped around him, the scent going deep inside and carrying away some of his anxiety. "Good afternoon," Obie said from the far side of the garden, where he was bent over a flower bed, a small pile of wilting weeds next to him. "My last appointment canceled, so I decided to get some work done out here since it's such a great afternoon."

"Wow," Bri said.

"What?" Obie turned to him, blinking.

"I thought the yellow hair was bright, but…." Obie's orange-red hair shimmered in the sun as if it had bits of fire in it. "How did you get that color, if I may ask?"

Obie put his hands to his hair as if he were trying to cover it up. "Oh God. I usually color it, but I've been experimenting a little and I haven't decided what I want to do with it. So, I let it grow out."

"It's…." Bri didn't have the words, but it didn't matter. It was so rare that he noticed anyone's hair color that he didn't really know what to say. "I like it."

24

Obie lowered his hands and stood up slowly. "I used to get teased a lot, so I started dying it when I was still in high school. I don't think it's actually been this color in years. I tried out the yellow, but didn't like it. And before that it was pink. I liked that, but it was a pain to maintain and didn't last very long."

Bri grinned. "Pink. That must have been bright."

Obie picked up the weeds and carried them to the back of the garden, returning a few moments later. "It was, but I wanted something unique. There must have been a dozen guys at the club last night with pink hair and even more with purple. I don't want to look like everyone else."

"Then be yourself. That guarantees you'll be different." Bri smiled, repeating the words his mother had told him when he'd begged to get his ears pierced as a teenager. She had threatened to beat his butt black-and-blue. She also told him if he came home with a tattoo, she'd skin him alive, so it would be gone anyway. Or so she'd said.

"You really like it?" Obie asked.

"I think it's amazing." Bri grinned and headed for the back door. Obie followed him inside and went right into the bathroom, washing his hands thoroughly.

"I see you wore shorts this time. That's good." Obie came out of the bathroom and closed the door. "Go ahead and hop up on the table. I want to get your muscles nice and relaxed before we go to work."

Bri got up on the table, and Obie set his crutches aside. "Do you go out to clubs like that—?" Bri started to ask, then groaned as Obie's hands began working his muscles. "God, I didn't realize how tight those muscles were until you got your hands on them." He sighed and closed his eyes, breathing deeply as relief warred with flashes of pain that diminished slowly.

"That's good. And to answer your question, I go out sometimes. The guys wanted to check out that club and they dragged me along. Not that it did either of them any good. I understand that both Chippy and David came home alone and ended up in the bathroom asleep before the porcelain throne before the night was over." He chuckled and continued working, his fingers getting deep into the muscles of

Bri's thigh. "They're not as tight as they were the last time. Have you been doing the exercises?"

"Yes, and I put a heating pad on a couple times a day." His words drifted off as Obie's magic hands made the pain he'd been living with slip away.

"Good. I'm going to massage your leg for a while, and then we'll get down to the real work of the day. I hate to say it, but you are going to be sore when we're done. But we need to get these muscles actually working again and retrained to take the weight properly." He continued his steady strokes, and Bri did his best not to moan. He knew he made the same sounds when he was having sex. Bri was already turned on and doing his best to ignore his half-awake dick. Instead, he tried to just focus on the pain relief.

"Okay. I'll do whatever you think is best." He raised his arms over his head, stretching his torso. "I'm putting myself in your hands." Bri tried to think of a time when he had ever said those words to anyone and he couldn't, at least not recently.

He closed his eyes, his mind drifting like it did when he got a massage. For some odd reason, his mind went back to his old friend, Billy Peterson. He hadn't thought of him in a very long time. He and Billy had lived on the same street and discovered they both felt the same way about other boys. At fifteen, they thought they knew everything, but of course, they actually knew nothing at all. Bri used to build forts; it was what the kids in the neighborhood did. He and Billy had scrounged up old pieces of wood and cobbled them together. One afternoon, they'd been bored and the two of them had ended up in the fort together, kissing, exploring. They didn't get very far, and afterward they both swore each other to secrecy. But the next time, they'd been caught by Billy's big brother. Bri had been sent home, and Billy had been sent away to camp for the rest of the summer, then enrolled in a private school. "Did you have gay friends growing up?" Bri asked without really thinking, his mind on Billy.

"That depends on what you mean. I had friends when I was in college. We used to march, or roll through pride parades on roller skates, wearing wings and carrying wands. The Rollerinas, we called each other, and we spread glitter wherever we went." Obie sighed. "Those were the days when we were carefree and didn't think anyone would hurt us."

Bri sat up, Obie's tone scaring him a little. "Who hurt you?" he growled, without meaning to.

He paused. "One of the sports guys, I'm afraid. He and some friends decided that they didn't like men like me having a good time. It was Philly Pride and we were in the parade." Obie's hands stopped, his palms resting on Bri's leg. Obie didn't even seem to realize what he was doing. "I knew him from a freshman class I had, and I think he followed us along the parade. And when it broke up at the end, he waited while we went in to change. He had a baseball bat." Obie's hands shook, and Bri thought he was going to be sick. "My friend, Harper, was in the hospital for a month. I was lucky—I got out to get help or, otherwise it would have been worse."

"What happened to him?"

"Harper was a brilliant artist. He had a stunning career ahead of him. The things he saw when he looked out the window would take your breath away." Obie began moving his hands again. "Now he spends most of his days sitting at a table coloring flowers with crayons he struggles to hold in his hands." A tear ran down Obie's face. "That asshole took away his future, his life, everything he was after the age of about nine."

"And the guy who hurt him?" Bri asked, remembering his own college years and the intolerance that sometimes prevailed in the locker room.

"He's in prison. They convicted him of a hate crime, and hopefully he'll never see the light of day again."

"Where did you go to school?" Bri asked, a chill racing up his spine. This story sounded way too familiar to him.

"I started college at Drexel." Obie turned away and resumed his work, rubbing his cheeks on his shoulders. "I'm sorry. This is very unprofessional of me. I shouldn't be acting this way." He stood a little straighter. "We should be using this time to talk about your knee and our plans for getting you into full-on basketball shape.

"Maybe." Bri put his hand on Obie's, stopping it. "I remember that incident. I was in the city and I knew him. Cooper Collins."

"Yeah. That was his name." Obie returned to work on his other leg.

Bri lay back down. "I played on the same team as him for a year. He was a freshman the same year I was a senior. A real asshole. He was one of those guys who thought he could build himself up by tearing others down. I didn't know him at the time that he hurt you and your friend, but I heard about the incident."

"Everyone did. They closed ranks around the athletes and defended them for weeks until everything came out. Meanwhile, Harper was in a coma and no one wanted to believe me. I ended up changing schools because of him. I couldn't take the harassment any longer. I transferred to Penn State and got my degree there." He pulled his hands away. "I think that's enough for now." Bri didn't know if he meant the massage, the topic of conversation, or both. Not that it mattered. Obie wiped his eyes again and stepped back.

"I understand. When I was in college, a guy on my floor, Willy, was hurt pretty badly." He paused, not really wanting to talk about it now. The air in the room was already thick enough that he didn't need to add to it. And from the slight puffiness around Obie's eyes, he didn't need to hear it. Bri wasn't up to talking about his grow-up moment anyway. "Why don't we get to work," he said around his slightly sore throat.

"Take off your shoes and carefully get off the table. I'm going to have you lie on the mat. We're going to work on some basic stretches. Carefully, with no quick movements. This is to get those muscles that you haven't been using ready to become functional again." Obie stood near his feet, looking at him, his eyes intensely meeting Bri's.

"How do we do this?" Bri lay flat on his back on the mat with Obie lifting his injured leg, cradling it in his hands.

"Okay. I want you to point your toes, stretching the muscles of your foot and upper leg. Hold it for a count of ten." There was a little discomfort. "Tell me if you experience pain. There might be some soreness or tightness that I hope will dissipate, but what we want to avoid is pain, sharp and damaging." Obie counted slowly. "Now release. Let's do it again." Three times, and then he stretched his foot the other way, tightening his calf. Three times he held it. "Now raise your leg at the hip, point your toes, and think long and strong. Feel it all the way down your leg."

"Wow," Bri said as he gritted his teeth. "I'm holding it as long as I can."

"Then relax and we'll do it some more times. I want you to hold it, make those muscles work for you. Don't bend your knee, just stretch and awaken your muscles," Obie said. He had a great voice—instructive, but encouraging in tone. It made Bri want to do whatever he asked, just because he didn't want to disappoint him. "Good. Now let's do both legs together. I know the other isn't injured, but your mind is getting used to having one leg and making do. So we need to retrain it to use both."

"Okay." Bri did it and found the injured leg had an easier time. Up and down, stretch and release. They worked his legs before even trying his knees. "Do you want me to try bending my knee with both legs together?"

"Now you're getting it. Don't go to the point of pain," Obie cautioned, and Bri bent his legs downward together. "Very good. A little more."

Damn, Bri's legs shook and sweat broke out on his forehead. Still, he pressed on, going slowly, with Obie guiding him with his magic hands. His abs ached from holding, taut and still. "I can't do any more." He straightened his legs and breathed deeply.

"That's good, but next time remember to breathe. You've worked out, so you know how to breathe for power. You have to do that here. Just because there aren't any weights involved, that doesn't mean you don't need that same control." Obie smiled. "That was awesome, by the way. You are already bending a little bit more than you did last time, though we have a lot of work yet to do."

Bri lay back, closing his eyes, praying to God to give him the strength to continue. He was already tired, sweating, and felt like he'd had a full workout. "One more?" Bri asked.

"At least four. Let's try it again."

Over and over they worked his knee, with no weight, just getting it moving. He hadn't even put any weight on it and already his leg felt more like his own than the part of him locked away in the brace.

"Okay, let's take a break." Obie got him a water. "Drink this and just breathe for a while. Let's rehydrate and oxygenate." Bri drained the bottle, then set it aside. A few minutes later, Obie was back at it, taking him through breathing exercises before going through the stretches, and more.

By the time Obie helped him back up and handed him his crutches, Bri was both energized and excited, as well as tired and wrung out. He knew he'd made real progress, and that felt good. "I know I'm going to be sore."

"Sore is good. Pain is not. Remember that. Drink lots of water and eat just like you would after a heavy workout, because you just had one. Your body is going to scream for energy and protein so it can heal. Be sure to give it what it needs. Stay lean, though."

"Damn. I was heading for onion rings. I'll have to go to Mediterranean Garden instead."

Obie chuckled. "Good choice." He chuckled, and his stomach rumbled. "I guess I need to eat as well."

Bri sat down and put his brace back on, hating the thing more and more each time he was able to take it off. For a while, it had felt protective, keeping out what might hurt him. But now, he found it restrictive, and he mentally chafed against it. "Do you want to join me?" Bri asked. "Unless you have another appointment or something."

"You're my last one. I try to keep Fridays lighter so I can make sure I'm caught up at the end of the week." He started closing down everything and turning off the lights. "Give me a few minutes and I'll go with you. As long as we understand that it's dutch treat." The caution in his eyes made Bri wonder if he'd had trouble with that sort of thing before.

"You got it. I'll finish up here and be ready when you are." He got the brace attached properly and then went through the process of getting his shoes on. It always took some doing, but he was ready to go when Obie returned. He followed him out, through the yard, passing both George and Gracie as they lounged in the shade near Obie's fountain.

"I'd offer to drive," Obie said. "But...." He opened the garage door, and Bri laughed outright at his Smart car. There was no way he was ever going to fit in that. "I only drive in town, and it sips gas." Obie closed the garage door, and Bri motioned to where his car was parked.

"It's no problem." Bri handed Obie his keys. "You go ahead and drive. It's probably better for my knee at this point, anyway. You'll get us there faster." And he needed food badly. He got into the car, and Obie did the same, moving the seat up and then setting the engine to purring.

"This is really awesome," Obie said, sliding back and forth over the seat. "I like my car because it's practical and good for the environment, but this is cushy. And it sure beats my bicycle seat."

"Bicycle?" Bri asked, trying to remember the last time he'd ridden one that wasn't in a gym.

"Yeah. I ride whenever I can, and on weekends I sometimes race, things like that. I like that I can lower my carbon footprint, making the world and our lives better. I only drive when I have to, really. My car is one of the first Smarts they imported. I've had it for, like, quite a while, and it has less than thirty thousand miles on it because I don't drive that often." He made a few turns. "Keep an eye out for parking, will you? It can be a pain this time of day."

"Right there." Bri grinned. He had great parking karma, and right now he was glad it was holding true. The car felt stuffy and close, even with the air-conditioning running. Bri knew it was his proximity to Obie—more importantly, the way his scent seemed to expand and fill the car. Each time he inhaled, he got a whiff of herbal freshness that tingled the back of his nose. It was probably a combination of the potion Obie used for massage, the plants he worked with, and his own fresh scent, sending Bri's olfactory nerves into a frenzy. Dammit, he nearly leaned closer just to get a stronger smell of it.

Obie parallel parked, and Bri opened the door. Before he could get his crutches, Obie brought them around for him and waited while he stood up. Then Obie handed him his keys, and they made their way down to the very busy restaurant.

"Mutasem," Obie said once they were inside, and a large man with black hair and a missing left eye hurried over to him. He also had a hand that was missing some fingers on the same side.

"Welcome, my friend," Mutasem said with a crooked smile that was warm and genuine, reaching all the way up his cheeks. "And my new friend. You were here last week. Welcome." He waved profusely. "I do not have a table right now."

"It's all right," a woman said from nearby. "We just sat down. Why don't you take our table and we can wait for the next one." She and a man Bri assumed to be her husband stood up, moving out of the way.

"Thank you. That's very nice of you," Obie said.

"I've been on crutches before," the woman said, as she walked back toward the waiting area. "It isn't fun."

At first Bri wondered if she and the man were being so nice because of who he was, but neither of them seemed to recognize him. Still, it was very thoughtful. "Obie, would you get a ball out of the trunk for me?" He handed him his keys and lowered himself into the chair, glad to be off his leg again. Obie had been right—the dull ache had already started.

"Is this what you wanted?" Obie said, once he'd come back from the car. He handed him the basketball, still in the box. Mutasem, obviously figuring out what was going on, came over with a marker. Bri signed the ball and dated it, then got up and took it over to the woman.

"Giving up the table was very kind. Please, take this as a thank-you." He smiled, and the woman seemed shocked. Her husband, on the other hand, grinned.

"That is so awesome. Our son is a huge fan and his birthday is next week. He's going to be thrilled." He shook Bri's hand profusely, and when another table opened up, they went over and were seated.

Obie sat down across from Bri. "That was pretty nice of you. I heard that a lot of guys only give autographs when they're paid to."

"Lots of them do. It's a whole other source of income. I did that for a while, but I found that giving a little of myself and being willing to meet the fans had its own rewards—ones that have nothing to do with money. After I got hurt, the team got hundreds of emails and even cards and letters wishing me a speedy recovery. Someone actually sent a tin of cookies, decorated as basketballs." He couldn't help smiling.

"I can see that. Being nice doesn't cost anything. But being liked helps in other ways."

"Yeah, it does. And it came back to me in a big way. I got endorsement deals because I was liked when other players were passed over." Bri worked hard to maintain his reputation. "I also don't go out and get drunk or make scenes. I only have so long to play, and once I'm not relevant anymore, the endorsements and other deals will fall away. How many athletes have you seen where everything gets ripped away because of a tweet or a picture of them doing something stupid? Remember Michael Phelps's bong pictures?" Bri shook his head slowly.

"I suppose. You're in the public eye and you have to act like it."

Bri nodded. "A lot of the guys didn't, and then they wondered why they were getting bad press or had people running after them all the time, trying to take pictures of whatever they were doing, just in case it could be sensationalized." Thankfully, for the most part, Bri's life off the court was boring enough that they rarely took an interest. And he wanted to keep it that way. "I love the game, I do. More than anything else, I'm happiest when I'm on the court. And I want to be able to keep doing that."

"Who's your hero?" Obie asked.

"Magic Johnson, I think. He was a great athlete and an incredible man both on and off the court."

Mutasem came over to the table. He talked for a few minutes as he explained what his specials were.

Obie turned to Bri. "Do you trust me?" Bri nodded, and Obie turned back to Mutasem. "Why don't you bring us what you think is best."

Mutasem grinned. "Wonderful."

"And we'll have water and your orange-carrot drinks." Obie shared a smile with Bri as Mutasem hurried away. "He's an amazing cook. Most of the dishes are variations on those his mother makes. Wait till you taste his tomato and cucumber dip." Obie rolled his eyes in bliss, and damned if Bri didn't wonder what it would be like to put that look on Obie's face… in a very different way. "He dices tomato and cucumber really small, adds some yogurt and tahini, garlic, and some other spices. You eat it on pita bread and it's tangy and zippy." He smacked his lips just as Mutasem brought fresh pita and the very dip he'd just mentioned. Bri took a bite and hummed right along with Obie. It was everything he'd described… and more.

"What's your dream?" Bri asked, getting their conversation back on topic.

"Oh goodness." Obie sighed and dipped another pita point. "I had so many of them. I was going to be a doctor, but that went out the window when I learned how long it took. There was no way I was ever going to be able to afford that much schooling. And I really like what I do." Obie smiled. "You know, if I had a dream, it would be to ride in the Tour de France. I do some races now and I like to think I'm pretty good."

"That's cool. Maybe once my knee is healed, we could ride together. I'm always looking for interesting ways to keep fit in the off-season. What else?" he asked, leaning a little closer. Obie had a way of knitting his brow just a little bit when he was thinking.

"I don't know if it qualifies as a dream, but I'd like to write a book on whole-life wellness." He sat up a little straighter and his eyes glinted with passion. "I really believe that the key to health is for all of us to look at our entire lives—what we eat, how we play, the spaces around us, the people we spend our time with, even the plants and animals that we allow to share our lives. It all impacts our health." He paused when Mutasem came over with small, lightly dressed salads. The lemon popped on his tongue, and Bri was suddenly even hungrier. "Even the friends you choose can impact your health," Obie continued.

"I can see that. Bad habits are so much easier to start than good ones and a hell of a lot harder to break."

Obie grinned. "Exactly. We are all influenced by the images and messages around us. I try to make it so that the ones around me are positive and help me live the way I want. That doesn't mean I always succeed, or that I'm a dick. At least I hope I'm not. I mean, it's important to listen to opposing viewpoints. That's not what I'm saying. But it's best to distance yourself from people who do things that aren't good for you."

"Like your feral friends?" It was too good a chance for him to pass up.

"Chippy and David are harmless. They're twinks—heck, so am I, I guess. They're over the top and love to have a good time. But when the chips are down, those guys are there for me like no one else ever has been." Obie turned, and Bri followed his gaze, the television over the counter catching his attention.

"You follow the Phillies?" Bri was a little surprised.

"I love sports. That's why I do what I do. After school, I wanted to go into athletic therapy. But jobs were hard to get, and I ended up at one of those huge practices with revolving doors of patients. One day I saw twenty people. *Twenty*. And I only got twenty minutes with each one of them, tops. I wasn't really helping them. When my grandpa died, he left me his house with the instructions that I sell it and use the money to make my life better. So I decided to start my own practice. That was three years ago, and Hunter was one of my first patients. I already knew Monty. I was able to help him, and he told everyone he knew. Word spread, and my clientele grew. Now, I stay as busy as I want to be. I work with athletes in baseball, football, hockey, soccer, rugby, basketball—you name it."

"I see." Bri finished his salad and sat back. It had been so good and incredibly light.

"Each sport has its own type of injuries," Obie continued. "I work with tennis players for arm and ankle injuries. They are really hard on themselves. Of course, I also do general work. I have a few patients who moved with me from the big practice. One lady had been seeing me for help with her back for years. There is nothing I can do to cure her, but I hope I make her life a little less pain-filled and help give her a better quality of life."

Obie was so different from most of the guys Bri knew. He got his pleasure from truly helping others, rather than from what they could do or how much money they made. And when he got excited, he waved his hands around and could barely sit still in his chair.

A server took their empty plates and returned with two bowls of rice-based dishes. One had meat in it, while the other seemed to be vegetable-based. "I believe that's a goat biriyani." Mutasem brought a third dish, also vegetarian, and placed it in the center of the table. It was majorly aromatic and contained fresh strawberries as well as nuts, raisins, and vegetables. Each dish looked amazing.

"I made some meat for your friend and vegetables for you," he said to Obie. "I hope you enjoy." He then made the rounds of the dining room, talking to the rest of his patrons while they filled their plates.

"This is so good," Bri moaned as he tasted the strawberry dish.

"It's a favorite of mine," Obie said. "Mutasem probably made it especially for us." He took a taste of his own. "I do love his cooking." Obie ate slowly as if savoring every taste, his lips closing around the tines of the fork so sensually.

Bri shifted his gaze downward. "I have to ask only because... well, I have to. Do you miss eating meat? I know I certainly would if I had to give it up."

"Maybe certain things. But if I were to try to eat it now in any quantity, my stomach would rebel. It's been long enough that it would be hard for me to digest." Obie leaned over the table. "I choose to live this way because it's healthier for me. I don't profess to have all the answers and I don't get on a soapbox to preach the doctrine of vegetarianism. Everyone gets to make their own choices. But sometimes I crave a BLT sandwich. They make bacon substitutes, but it just isn't the same." He added the last part in a whisper.

"Do you have them often?" Bri asked, with a little smile. He loved that Obie could tease and let him in on little secrets about himself.

"No. But when I do, I get good sourdough bread, fresh lettuce and tomato, and make the best BLT I can. I can only eat one sandwich. Any more and it's too much, so I make it a good one." He licked his lips, and Bri stifled a groan as Obie's pink tongue traced the outline of his lips. "The last time I had one was months ago. Though you're making me hungry for one." He chuckled lightly.

"I don't get them much either. I eat lean and healthy myself—chicken, fish, lots of vegetables and whole grains. We have team trainers who help us eat right. Otherwise, there's no way we'd make it through a game."

"What do you do before a game? I always find the different things athletes do interesting." He took another bite, and for a second, Bri forgot what he was going to say. He stuck a forkful of food into his own mouth to cover up his gaffe and give himself a chance to remember without looking like a fool.

"Old-fashioned carb loading. I eat a lot of pasta the day before to get plenty of energy running through my system. It all depends on the timing of the game. I try to avoid heavy proteins until after the game is over. Then I eat quite a bit to recover. The team schedule during the season is demanding, and it takes a lot of energy in order to be able to play at my peak, day after day, week after week. I'm sure it's the same for a lot of athletes."

Obie nodded. "Yes. I tend to do the same thing before bicycle races. I have to get my body primed for the energy expenditure. That's one of my real areas of interest. I ride bikes, but I don't make my living with my body or my athletic prowess, so I didn't know if it was different."

Bri nodded. "In some ways it is, and in others it isn't. I have access to resources that most people don't. Like you." He blew air out of his mouth. "There's also some pretty ugly stuff. Professional sports are not for the faint of heart." Bri stopped. He wasn't going to go into a discussion of the darker side of the business he was in. Not that he didn't know about the pressure and the lure of better performance through chemistry, but that wasn't good dinner conversation.

Bri turned toward the door as a man came into the restaurant. He didn't know what made him turn around other than the hair on his neck standing up. "Well, well," Donald Mitchell said as he made a beeline to their table. "What do we have here?"

Bri shivered just from the guy's tone. Donald was a team member, third-string, barely holding on, and yet he managed to stick around by the skin of his teeth. Bri had no idea why the team kept him. He wasn't a particularly great player and he stirred the drama pot at every opportunity.

"Donald, this is my physical therapist, Obie. He and I were working this afternoon and we decided to grab some food afterward." Damn it all, he shouldn't need to explain anything to this asshole, and it pissed him off that he felt he had to.

"Pleased to meet you," Obie said gently, his eyes narrowing slightly, flashing Bri a questioning glance. He held out his hand, but Donald ignored it. Obie might have muttered something about rudeness and then returned to his dinner.

"What do you need?" Bri asked, not hiding his impatience. Donald thought he was better than everyone else. It didn't matter what his performance was on the court; in his mind, he was the best and no one was going to change his opinion. To the rest of the world, he came across as a snobbish, smug asshole. "Were you stopping in for dinner?" He knew damn well Donald would never eat in a place like this. The owner didn't fit Donald's narrow-minded worldview.

He scrunched his face as if he'd just sucked a lemon. "No. But I was passing by and saw you in here." Donald leaned close. "You should watch the places you go and the people you're with. People might get the wrong idea." His words sounded like something out of a bad TV movie. Bri's mouth hung open for a second.

"And what idea is that? I like to eat? That I have friends who might want to eat with me? I can see where *certain people* might find that a foreign concept." He had to get the dig in there. Donald always rubbed him the wrong way—he wasn't the brightest bulb on the string.

"This place, run by foreigners and extremists," Donald stage-whispered.

Bri shook his head and went back to his food. He took another bite and turned to Obie, who looked at Donald as though he'd grown a second head. "Do you really believe something that completely stupid? Because if you do, I pity you," Obie said, his lips turned downward. "That's just sad."

Bri had to stifle a laugh, because Donald had turned bright red, as if the top of his head was about two seconds from blowing off. "You pity me?" He whirled back around to face Bri. "What kind of people are you spending time with?"

Bri had had enough. "Ones who are a hell of a lot smarter than you. Now go, before I have you thrown out." He smiled. "And I will be having a discussion with management about this little incident. They won't take kindly to this type of talk." He shook his head, turning away to go back to his lunch.

Reacting quickly to what Bri didn't see coming, Obie jumped out of his seat, the chair falling back. By the time Bri turned around, Obie had Donald by the wrist, twisting his arm around, pressing it upward behind his back. "He was going to coldcock you."

"Should I call the police?" Mutasem asked.

"No. I'll get him out of here." Obie maneuvered Donald to the door and pushed him out. Donald was bigger, but Obie proved that smarts and a little know-how could lick brawn every time. Obie and Mutasem stood at the door until Donald left. Bri set down his fork, not hungry any longer.

"Where did you learn to do that?" Bri asked when Obie sat back down, snapping his napkin and placing it back on his lap.

Obie smiled. "I'm a gay kid who was out in high school. I'm also smaller, so guys thought they could pick on me. I learned to fight quick and dirty. I have no qualms about going for any sensitive areas. The quicker I was able to put a guy on the ground, the faster I could get away and go for help. If this guy had given me any trouble, he'd be singing soprano, and not the kind on TV." Obie returned to his diner as though nothing had happened.

"Thanks. He could have really hurt me." Bri rubbed the back of his neck. "I shouldn't have turned away from him like that."

"You had no way of knowing how loose his bolts were. You need to tell your team about this. I'll talk to them, if I have to. That guy is going to hurt someone—maybe himself, though one less moron in the world isn't necessarily a bad thing." Obie ate some more, and Bri sat, watching him. "Don't let Donald the Dick ruin your dinner," Obie added. "You need to eat, and this is so good."

Bri agreed. He wasn't going to let Donald win, but he also watched Obie. People didn't surprise him all that often, but Obie sure seemed to have hidden depths. "That guy just frosts my butt."

Obie snickered. "I could tell. Is he always that obnoxious?"

"Yes. He thinks he's the thought and behavior police. Everyone should feel the same way he does about everything, and he never shuts the hell up about it. The rest of the team tends to ignore him, but Donald takes that as agreement, which only encourages him. I argue with him sometimes, but the other guys just shake their heads and I end up standing alone." He set down his fork. "Most of the guys just want to play and not make waves, I get that. But there are times when you have to stand up for what you believe in. Especially when it comes to this guy's brand of superiority."

"Huh. I would have thought that with the team makeup, he'd get no traction on that kind of crap." Obie ate the last bite on his plate and sighed contentedly. Damn, that sound was mesmerizing, and once again Bri forgot what he wanted to say, lost in Obie's flaming red hair and deep blue eyes.

"Sorry," he said and willed his head back on track. "Donald is pretty careful about who he talks to, but sometimes he goes too far."

Obie shook his head. "I'm sorry. It sucks when you have a coworker who's a pain in the ass. I had this guy at my first job—he'd been there for like ten years and thought he was the senior therapist. He tried to be everyone's boss and thought he should get his pick of the patients. The thing was, they didn't like him. So a lot of repeat

patients would ask for someone *other* than him, and it pissed him off."
Obie grinned and leaned across the table. "Once, I was working with
a patient, one that he had worked with before. She hadn't been getting
anywhere with him, but with me, she was seeing progress. Anyway,
he accused me of poaching his clients. And he did it loudly enough
that she heard."

"Oh lord…," Bri murmured in anticipation.

"Yup. She told him off, right in the middle of the open therapy
room. She told him he was as useful as tits on a boar and that she had
gotten more help from me in a few weeks than she ever got from him."
Obie grinned. "As far as I know, he's still there, making everyone's
life miserable."

"Why?" Bri asked.

"His uncle owns the practice and I think he's too scared to fire
him. He should, though." Obie sighed. "I found the best way to deal
with a guy like that was to do my best and let him make a fool of
himself. It took a few months, but he did it in spades. I'm willing to
bet Donald will self-destruct on his own. He almost did tonight." Obie
stopped talking as Mutasem returned to their table.

"The food was amazing," Bri told him. "Thank you."

"Only the best," he said, putting his hands together and bowing
slightly with a wide smile.

"I loved your food," Bri told Mutasem. "Thank you for another
great meal." He waited until he left before getting out his wallet and
passing Obie some bills.

"It's too much," Obie said, handing some back.

"Add it to the tip. A meal like that deserves to be rewarded."
Obie took care of the bill, and they left the restaurant together, going
to his car. He looked around, half expecting to see Donald come
lumbering up the street. Thankfully, he wasn't around. Bri was able
to get into the car in peace, and Obie drove them back to his house.

"That was fun… well, except for Donald. Then again, sometimes
it can be entertaining to pick on the stupid." Obie grinned. "I know it's
wrong, but sometimes people like that…."

"It was fun, but I'm doing my best to try to forget about him."
Bri ground his teeth together. "You saw the tape that showed me
getting hurt, so you know he was involved. It was supposed to be a
charity game, something we do to raise money for the Boys and Girls
Club. It's fun—we get to play and mess around. They call it a game,
but it's really a day to put on a little bit of a show and spend some
time with the kids. We bring balls, and the team sponsors giveaways,
stuff like that."

"I've been to one of those events. It was super fun, and you guys
looked like you were having a ball."

"I was, until Donald got all huffy after he flubbed a few shots in
front of everyone. He became aggressive, and that changed the tenor
of the game. Suddenly both sides were really starting to go for it—at
least that's how I remember it. I was still playing like it was a charity
game and I'm the one who got hurt." He was more than a little bit
bitter. "It was so stupid."

"It always is, until someone gets hurt." Obie turned off the
engine and got out. "Thanks for a great dinner." He smiled and waited
while Bri got out, then went around to the other side of the car. It took
Bri a while to maneuver, but he was getting a little better.

He got his crutches stowed and started the engine, lowering his
window. "I promise I'll do my exercises. Did we set up appointments
for next week?"

"Tuesday and Friday at two," Obie answered. "I'll see you
then." Bri waved and backed out about a foot before coming to a stop.

"The team has an exhibition game on Sunday and I have some
extra tickets. Would you like them? You probably have plans, but if
you're free, it could be fun. I've got four tickets." He stifled a cringe
as he thought of Obie's feral friends, then shrugged. He was a big guy
and he could take it. "Bring your friends, if you like. These things are
always better with people you know."

Obie gave him one of those "are you sure?" looks. "Why don't
you invite your friends? Don't get me wrong—I'd love to go, and I'm
sure Chippy and David would enjoy themselves, but…."

"Most of my friends will be there already. They'll be playing while I sit on the bench and watch." That was the real shits about these things. He was expected to be there, to be seen and to support the team, but it ate him alive because he wanted to be out there with the rest of the team.

"I'll call the guys and tell them. I think it would be awesome." He grinned from ear to ear, as if he'd just been told he got a second Christmas morning this year. "Count me in, and I'll confirm with the others and tell them to be on their best behavior."

"Awesome." Bri liked that Obie would be there with him. "I'll call you tomorrow with the details." He left it at that and rolled up the window, backing out and heading for home.

He was just pulling into his driveway when his phone rang. He checked out the number on the car display and denied the call. It read as Number Blocked, so it was most likely a telemarketer. He hated those guys, but sometimes they were a fact of life. As he got out of the car, his phone chimed, letting him know he had a voice message. Bri figured he'd listen to the very beginning of it and delete it if it was useless.

"You don't listen very well, Bri," the message began. "You taint the sport by your company and who you are seen with, and that club… is a blemish on the city and the sport you play. I sent a message. You didn't listen. This next time I won't be so subtle. If you won't listen, maybe your friends will have to help you. Maybe they need to feel some pain. Then you'll change your ways."

Bri leaned against the car, listening to the second message once again. He had no idea who it was, though the voice was familiar. Bri ran through the message twice more, just listening to the voice. If he had to guess, given the kind of message it was, he'd have thought Donald was behind this, but it definitely wasn't his voice.

He saved the message and wondered if he should call the team or the police. He'd gotten crank calls before, and the last time he'd just gotten a new cell number. That had been such a hassle, and he didn't want to do it all over again. But then maybe it was necessary. There were times when he loved his job. Playing basketball was all he'd ever wanted to do, and he'd led his team to several successful seasons. That had been amazing, the best time ever. But sometimes, especially at times like this, being in the public eye was a huge pain in the butt. Bri decided he'd call the team and get their advice when he got a chance.

I HATE it when people ignore me. I sent the message loud and clear. Maybe Bri Early isn't as smart as he likes to think he is. I put the burner phone down on the table and sit down. I need to think. One way or another, he is going to pay. I get to my feet once again, pacing the small, dingy room like a caged tiger. Yeah that's it—I'm in a cage, one built by Bri Early, and I need to get out. *Think*, I remind myself. I need to figure out how I'm going to get my message across. A deep breath in and out soothes me and I stop pacing. Time. I have time and I'll figure it out. Then the damn closet case asshole is going to pay.

CHAPTER 4

"WE'RE REALLY going to a basketball game?" Chippy asked as he pulled open Obie's closet. "What does one wear to this kind of sporting event?" He put on a fake English accent that made him sound especially stupid.

Obie reached inside, flipping a Rockets jersey off the hanger. "You can wear this—you'll fit right in."

Chippy turned to show the shirt to David. "Would you wear this? It looks like I have a dildo on my chest. A weird-shaped one, but it's definitely a sex toy." He made a squeal. "I wonder if they sell those in the fan shops. Do you think I could order them as Christmas presents?" He pranced around the bed and flopped down, laughing himself silly at his own stupid joke.

"Be nice," David said. "This could be fun, and I think Obie has a thing for this guy. Bri must like him if he gave us tickets—even though he likely knew he'd bring you." David tapped Obie on the shoulder. "Are you sure he knows what he's getting himself in for?"

"I promised him you two would be less feral than at the club. Man, you just about scared him senseless." His friends could be over the top sometimes, but they always put a smile on his face. And when push came to shove, they had his back, without question.

David put his hands on his hips in fake indignation. "Well, I saw him first and you totally cockblocked me. But I'll forgive you." He made a big production of waving some imaginary wand. As long as he wasn't shaking the one that came attached, Obie counted himself good.

"You two need to go home and get ready." He set out his other jersey, the one he intended to wear. "Be back here in half an hour and ready to go. I'm not going to wait for you. Bri has to go in early because he needs to sign autographs and make sure he's there to be

45

seen by the fans. But he said he'd join us at game time." Obie was more than a little nervous.

"Don't worry. We'll be good." Chippy picked up the jersey and they left his room, closing the front door to the house on their way out. Obie started the shower for a quick cleanup so he wouldn't smell like lotion and the garden. Then he styled his hair and made sure his face was presentable before slipping on a T-shirt, then the jersey over it and a pair of jeans that he knew made his backside look completely doable. He took a look in the mirror and almost changed into a different pair. This was a sporting event. And even though Bri was as hot as a bonfire on steroids, they had gone out once as friends—that was all. He had no reason to think there was anything between them. Besides, Bri was a client, and Obie was not going to get into any of those ethical gray areas. Starting a relationship with him would be unprofessional and could only end badly.

The door opened as Chippy and David clamored inside. "We're ready. Are you?" Chippy chimed up the stairs.

"I'm ready, Miss Thing," he answered as he hurried down.

"Well, damn…," David said as he gave him the once-over. "For someone who professes that you're only friends with this guy, that he's just a client, you're wearing your metronome pants."

"I am not, whatever the hell that means." Obie rolled his eyes in an overdramatic fashion.

Chippy giggled. "It means those damn things are so tight that when you walk, your ass slides from side to side. If you were a train, you be saying, 'fuck me, fuck me, fuck me, choo choo.'" He pulled his arms down to imitate blowing a train whistle.

"Then I need to change." He knew it. He should have just worn an old pair of jeans rather than these newer ones.

"No time, honey," David countered. "We need to go now. There's an accident on the road into the city and we are never going to get around it if we don't leave right now." He already had the door open and was making shooing motions. "Let's get out of here." He stepped out the back door and hurried out to where he'd parked his Fiesta. It wasn't much bigger than Obie's Smart car, but it did have a tiny back seat. Since he'd gotten the tickets, that meant Chippy was the lucky one crammed in the back.

They no sooner got the doors closed than David zipped out of the alley and down to the street, practically cutting off three people as he made the turn. The man was a menace on the road, and Obie held the oh-shit handle and prayed until they got onto the freeway and came to a stop a mile later. Then, and only then, could he breathe again, but only because there was no place to go.

It took half an hour before they passed the accident, and then Obie wondered if they were going to be involved in one of their own as David floored it, weaving in and out of traffic until they got through downtown and pulled up in front of the stadium. Man, he'd never been so damned happy to get anywhere as he was when they turned into the parking lot. Obie leaned over the seat, handing the attendant the pass Bri had given him. They were motioned around the lines of cars waiting to park and zipped up to the front into a reserved section before sliding into a spot.

"Now that's what I call a parking space." David puffed up enough that you'd have thought the preferential treatment was because of him. Obie didn't disabuse him of that notion and pointed toward the nearest door. "That's where we need to go."

"Are you sure?" David asked, seeing the two huge men on either side of it. "They'll snap us like twigs." He sounded a little frightened and turned on at the same time. David definitely had a type, and it corresponded to the guy on the left, who had blond hair, a surfer's tan, and arms that filled his T-shirt. The other man, with his dark hair, was more Chippy's type, but the perpetual sneer on his lips was probably going to keep him away.

"Yes, Bri said to enter here." Obie marched right up to the door and showed the men the tickets that Bri had messengered to him. The blond looked him over, his eyes widening, and then handed him back the tickets. The other guy looked at them as well, sharing a glance with his compatriot before motioning them inside with a crisp movement. Obie went straight through with Chippy, while David lingered for just a few seconds before following behind them. "It's right up here."

Obie pointed and led them up to an entrance, and then, following the seat layout, down closer to the front. Another man stood at a gate of sorts, and Obie showed him their tickets.

"Gentlemen," he said gently, opening the gate. "Wait here, please."

Obie stood off to the side, waiting until he came back. "Holy crap," David whispered. "No wonder they looked at us like we were from another planet."

Obie glanced around at the men all sitting there, looking at them as if they were an exhibit in the zoo. Most were wearing jerseys and jeans, and some had scruffy beards. These were guys, regular guys. Certainly none of them wore eyeliner or a touch of sparkle above the eyes. Some even curled their lips upward or turned away to talk to the guy next to them. Obie lifted his head, turned toward where the man had gone, and waited. There was no way he was going to give anyone the satisfaction of seeing him react to them.

"Obie," Bri said as he made his way over on his crutches. "Come on through."

"Bri Early?" one of the men asked, hurrying forward with his hand extended. Suddenly the other men were up from their seats, with more following behind. Bri shook hands with each one and smiled, taking a few minutes and signing some autographs.

"Excuse me, guys, I need to get off my feet," he told the gathering crowd, and backed inside the enclosure. Obie joined him with David and Chippy, and then the gate was closed and Bri slowly made his way back to where he'd been sitting. "Did you have any trouble?"

"No," Obie answered. "You remember David and Chippy."

"Of course." Bri motioned to four chairs right at the edge of the court, maybe ten feet from where the other players sat. Obie got the guys seated and then took the chair next to Bri.

"This is something," Obie said, his left foot bouncing on the floor. Some of the other players approached to speak with Bri, and he introduced them all. Obie was in heaven.

"Sam Griffith," Obie said as a tall man approached, his bright smile contrasting with his dark skin.

"Sam, this is Obie," Bri said. David and Chippy were deep in their own conversation by this time. "He's helping me get back on my feet. Sam is—"

"The best forward in the league, in my opinion," Obie said, a little starstruck. "The way you thrust yourself into the air is a thing of beauty." The much bigger man's hand engulfed Obie's as he shook it.

"I'm glad you think so," Sam said.

"In the game against Boston last year, I thought you were never going to come down at that toss-up. It was amazing." Sam was known for his ability to hang in the air, defying gravity for that fraction of a second that it took to give him the edge. "I love watching you and Bri play. It's amazing." Obie could barely contain himself as a whistle blew and Sam excused himself to join the rest of the team.

"You know your stuff," Bri said.

"I'm a huge fan." He stood and showed Bri the back of his jersey with the name Griffith emblazoned on the top. "David is wearing the one I have with your name on it." The teams filed out onto the court and the players were introduced, waving to the crowd and putting on a short shooting exhibition. The Washington Governors did the same thing as they were introduced, to the delight of the crowd.

"See Rogers over there," Obie said, leaning close to Bri. "He's nursing his left arm a little."

"How can you tell?" Bri asked.

"Watch him shoot. It's good, but he's compensating, and his right arm is going to ache by the end of the evening." Obie smiled as the players lined up for the start of the match.

"This is only an exhibition game, so the guys should be having fun as long as no one does something stupid to get the others going. Donald isn't playing. He was specifically uninvited to ensure there'd be no repeat of last time." Bri seemed pleased.

Once the national anthem was sung, the game got under way.

"Guys, just watch, this is really cool," Obie whispered to David and Chippy.

49

"Oh, we're watching," David cocked one eyebrow. "There's so much to see." Obie knew his friend was more interested in the players than the actual game.

"I meant the game," Obie hissed.

"You watch your ball game and we'll watch ours," Chippy retorted, and Obie stifled a groan, figuring he'd leave his friends to have their own fun, focusing his attention on the contest in front of him.

"This is so awesome," Obie said, turning to Bri. "Thanks for inviting us. It's a once-in-a-lifetime thing for me." He jumped to his feet as Sam scored a three-pointer, clapping, jumping, and yelling at the top of his lungs. He sat back down as play resumed, and one of the Rockets stole the ball, heading back downcourt, passing it to Sam, who did a repeat. "Damn, that was smooth."

"It's what Sam does," Bri said, with a hint of disappointment. "I should be out there."

He bumped Bri's shoulder lightly. It was as intimate a gesture as he dared in a setting like this, but his heart felt for him. Obie knew what it felt like to be on the outside looking in on things he wanted, but couldn't have. "I know. We'll get you back to playing condition just as soon as we can." The Rockets scored big again and were pulling ahead.

At the end of the first period, the Rockets were in the lead, and the players were having a ball, by the look of things. The Rockets took their seats and one of the officials wheeled a rack of basketballs onto the court. "What's this?" David asked.

"Hoop shoot for charity," Bri answered. "Each shot is a hundred dollars. If you make it, you get a team-signed ball." He pulled out a red ticket and handed it to Obie. "Go for it."

"You want me to shoot?"

"Yeah, Obie, go win yourself a ball," David teased.

"Do you want to try?" Bri asked David and Chippy, who both shook their heads.

Obie leaned close to Bri. "They're only good with balls that are attached."

Bri rolled his eyes. "Then head on out and get in line. It goes fast." Obie stood and went right onto the court. It almost felt as though he was stepping onto hallowed ground, following the crowd of kids and adults as they lined up on either side of the court.

Sam stood near him, with other home-team players spread out to watch. It added to the excitement and pressure of trying to make that single shot.

"Well, what do you know. If those jeans were any tighter and that walk a little lighter, you'd float up to the basket, princess." The asshole standing in line behind him knocked Obie lightly, just to let him know he was talking about him. Obie didn't turn around and ignored the guy. "Hey, princess, can you even throw a ball?" He knocked Obie harder, and he had to take a few quick steps to catch his balance.

Obie turned to face the idiot and found Bri hobbling his way across the court. "Sam, this guy doesn't get to shoot," Bri said, pointing and glaring at the asshole. "Take him out of line for being unsportsmanlike."

"Hey—" The guy turned and came face to face with a six-foot-six, pissed-off basketball player. "I paid my money."

Bri took a crutch step closer. "Then take your shot and stop running your mouth or you will be removed from the stadium." The line moved, and Bri stayed with Obie in line.

"You don't need to do that. I can take care of myself. He was all mouth and shoved like a girl." Obie raised his voice a little. "Only bullies pick on people smaller than them." Obie turned, glaring at the asshole until they reached the front of the line. "You go first," he said, dramatically stepping aside. "Let's see you do it." He crossed his arms over his chest. "I bet you can't shoot for crap."

Bri backed away as the man stepped to the free throw line. "One shot, from here," the attendant said, handing the unkempt bearded guy with greasy hair the ball.

"Do you ever back down?" Bri asked.

"You have to fight stupid somehow." Obie waited as the guy took his shot, the ball hitting the rim and bouncing right back at him. The attendant caught the ball and motioned for the asshole to step aside.

"You can do it," Bri said, and Obie stepped up. The attendant said his piece, and Obie stood on the line, glanced at the idiot who was watching him, and shot, clear and easy. The ball moved through the air, arced, and then… swish, nothing but net. "That's awesome," Bri told him as Obie was handed his autographed ball. He made eye contact with the asshole and then turned away, walking with Bri back to their seats.

"You're good with the unattached kind of balls too." Chippy was still jumping up and down in excitement when Obie returned. David seemed about ready to wet himself.

"I'm not just a pretty face, you know." He flashed a satisfied grin to each of them and then turned to the people behind him. About five rows up, a little girl in a wheelchair sat next to the aisle. Obie went up and handed her the ball. She was probably about six or seven, with deep brown eyes and a crooked smile that lit her face. "Honey, would you like this?" She took it, holding it to her with a grin that lit up the entire place.

"Are you serious?" her dad asked from next to her. "What do you say, Kimmy?"

"Thank you," she said, still hugging the ball.

"You're welcome." Obie shook hands with her dad and was about to go back down.

"Kimmy and I watch basketball together all the time. We have since I could hold her on my lap. She really wanted to go out there and shoot." The part about her not being able to was understood.

"I'm glad she's happy. Enjoy the rest of the game." Obie turned and took his seat again.

"You were on the JumboTron," David said and pointed as they replayed the clip where Obie gave Kimmy the ball. The caption underneath read "Play of the night." Obie swallowed and turned away.

"I didn't do it for that. I mean, I would have liked the ball, but it's going to mean a lot more to a child than it is to me," he said softly.

"That's why it's special," Bri told him as he bumped his shoulder. "You did something kind because that's who you are." He turned, and Obie tried to read his expression. Regardless, it sent a river of heat running down his back and made him wonder just what was going through Bri's mind. Obie hadn't thought this was a date—at least he hadn't thought that was his intention—but it was sure feeling that way. And he had worn these pants, which were tight enough to cut off the circulation to his legs if he didn't sit right. So there was that. But Bri hadn't mentioned that this was anything other than a night out as a thank-you for his help. Still, the way Bri looked at him sometimes, with heat and longing in his eyes, tugged at Obie's heart. Because underneath, he saw fear, cold and hard, just waiting to spring forward.

The basket-shooting ended and the second half got underway. Only now, the seriousness of the first half seemed to have disappeared. This was about grown men showing off. Trick shots abounded, and both teams seemed to forget about any sort of game and just had fun. It was a joy to watch. "He's looking at you again," David whispered when the crowd clapped to cover his voice.

"Who?" Obie asked.

"Bri," David said with a wink. "Every time you turn away, he watches you, and when you turn back, he's suddenly interested in the game." He nudged Obie's shoulder. "You know, maybe I should ask him his intentions. I am your best friend, and I need to know he isn't going to mistreat you or just use you." David sat back as Obie stifled a cough. "Because if he just wants to use someone, I'm definitely available."

Obie choked, and Bri gently patted his back. One of the guys tossed a bottle of water their way, and Bri caught it, offering it to him. "You okay?" Thank God he hadn't heard any of that little exchange.

"Yes." He sipped some of the water and used the bottle as cover to glare at David. Once he settled down, he took another drink, getting comfortable and watching the rest of the game, though he found himself glancing at Bri out of the corner of his eye just to see if he was indeed watching him. David might have been telling the truth, but then again, it was hard to tell. So Obie gave up, watching the fun until the timer ran out and the game ended. The players all shook hands and headed off the court as the spectators filed out toward the exits.

"Do we get to go into the locker room or something?" Chippy asked. "I mean, we got to sit down front and all. So, we should get to do that too."

David smacked him on the shoulder before Obie got a chance to do it. "Behave. You don't get to ogle the players as they change. That isn't included in the ticket... though it is something I'd definitely pay for."

"Stop gossiping like old ladies," Obie chastised the guys. "No, you don't get to go in the locker room to see everyone's business. How would you like it if I opened up your bathrooms? Those men would be shocked at the gels, mousses, creams, glitter, makeup, and God knows what all they'd find in any of them."

Bri had stopped ahead of them, and he glanced back, thankfully amused. At least the guy wasn't running for the hills, though that could come later. "Do you really have all that stuff?" he asked, in what Obie could only describe as complete disbelief.

"Of course," David said, striking a pose as others shifted around him at the top of the stairs. "Do you really think nature gave us everything you see?" He shook his head. "God, no. It takes hours for us to look this good. We have to wash, primp, tease, comb, color, gel, and style... and that's just our hair."

"Hold it there, Paul Mitchell. That's enough. Bri doesn't need to know all this." God, it was going to scare the man all to hell. "Let's just say that our bathrooms are full of product, and as we get older, we collect more and more of it." He caught up with Bri. "You, on the other hand, look great." He wanted to trace that little line across Bri's forehead. It made him look distinguished. "You have one of those faces like Sean Connery's. The older you get, the better you're going to look. Now, me? God... I'm just glad you haven't seen my uncle Jeremiah. I'm going to look just like him, I know it."

David snickered as they reached the exit door and were about to go outside. "Oh, stop it. Your uncle smoked like a fish for most of his life and he drank—ouch." He moved away from Chippy. "Don't elbow me."

"Then keep your mouth shut." Chippy rolled his eyes.

Obie shook his head slowly at both of them. "If there was a vice possible, my uncle became a connoisseur. He smokes like a chimney, drinks like a fish, and screws like a mink, with everyone he isn't married to. I saw him three years ago, and I know he's living in Vegas now. Mom hasn't had anything to do with him in years, but he'd show up like a bad penny every once in a while, trying to get her to help him out." Obie stumbled over a loose mat edge as they stepped outside. Bri grabbed him, and Obie regained his balance. "Sorry about that. As I was saying, Mom and Dad are great, but I wasn't particularly lucky in the extended family department. Especially since everyone says I look like my uncle. It's like my parents had no genetic input." He didn't want to talk about this, but now that it had been brought up…. "You'd like my mom and dad, and I'd bet they'd love to meet you sometime. But as for the rest of my family…." He sighed. "It's best if you don't dip too heavily in that gene pool."

"At least your dad is hot," Chippy chimed in.

"Yeah, way hot," David added his two cents. "For an older guy, I'd do him."

Obie coughed loudly as Chippy again smacked David on the back of the head. "Way too much information."

David rubbed the back of his head. "I was only being honest."

"Guys," Bri interrupted. "Ever heard of TMI—too much information?" They'd obviously had one too many beers during the game and it was loosening their tongues more than usual. Thankfully, they grew quiet, and Obie was able to walk the rest of the way with Bri to the parking area in relative peace.

"We should call it a night and get these two home." Obie looked over his shoulder and found David and Chippy already on their way to the car a few rows back. He turned to Bri, shifting his weight on his feet. "Thank you for everything. It was a great night." He still wasn't sure if this was a date, and under different circumstances, he would have kissed Bri good night. He wasn't used to this kind of uncertainty. Was Bri even interested in him? He sure acted like it, and the guys thought so too. Chippy and David were many things, but their gaydar was almost perfect.

"Are you okay to get to the car?" Bri asked. He didn't turn away and his gaze met Obie's in a rush of heat, but he didn't come any closer. Some sort of sign would be good, but whatever Bri was thinking, he wasn't giving anything away.

"For God's sake, just kiss him," David shouted across the cars.

Obie rolled his eyes. "I'm sorry about that." It was definitely time to go after that bit of embarrassment. "I'll get those two home before they embarrass the entire city of Philadelphia. Be sure to rest your leg, and I'll see you on Tuesday." He turned and headed for David's car. A row over, he turned back and saw Bri watching him. Obie waved, and Bri returned it. Then he picked up the pace and reached the car. "Not a single word from either of you or, I swear to God, I'll make you both walk home." He glared at each of them before unlocking the car.

Thankfully, both of the guys took him at his word, and neither of them said a thing as he started the engine and drove through the city.

"Can we talk now?" David asked, the first to crack. "You should have just kissed him. He wanted you to, I could tell. He had that desperate look in his eyes like he wanted it, but didn't know how to go about getting it. If anyone is going to make the first move, it'll have to be you."

"Then there won't be any moves made. He's a client and a friend. There is such a thing as ethics, you know."

"There's also such a thing as hiding behind all that stuff to keep from putting yourself out there. He's an amazing guy, and I don't get the feeling like he's just out to get into your pants. If he was, he'd be all pushy and in your face. He isn't. This is a quality guy."

Obie pulled to a stop at a light just before getting on the freeway. "You don't even know if he's gay."

"He is. Without a doubt. No one can look at another guy the way he looked at you and not be gay," Chippy chimed in from where he was splayed out in the back seat, his eyes closed. "That man wants you." He hiccupped.

"Great, just what I needed. Advice to the lovelorn from Miller and Bud, matchmakers." His friends had definitely had more to drink than they should have, but they were having fun. And since he was driving, there was no harm in it.

"Pick all you want, but it's true. I saw it too. And I really think Bri is gay. He was at the club that night, and he keeps looking at you like you're an all-you-can-eat buffet and he's starving. Also, he was as close to kissing you as you were to kissing him. So next time you get the chance, do it and see what happens. Who knows? It may be complete dullsville, and if that's the case, you can walk away and laugh it off. But—"

"There is no but," Obie broke in.

"Oh, there was a butt," Chippy slurred. "I got a look at it as he was leaving. And man oh man, I could get down and pray to a butt like that." He groaned slightly as Obie slowed down with traffic.

"If you got down on your knees with him, it wouldn't be to pray, I can tell you that," David retorted as he leaned into the back seat. "And yes, I agree." He sat facing forward again. "That was definitely a world-class butt. You should take a few seconds to get a handful of it when you do finally get a lip-lock on Bri."

Obie growled under his breath. "That's enough, guys. There aren't going to be any kisses or lip-locks. He's a friend and a client and that's all there is to it."

Chippy snorted. "I think he doth protest too much."

"Oh for God's sake," Obie groaned.

Chippy chuckled as though he'd won some kind of prize, and then after a minute the sound changed to soft snores. The alcohol must have finally kicked in for both of them, because the car grew quiet. Obie had never been so thankful for two sleeping drunks in his life. Now he could worry about them instead of having thoughts of Bri, his lips, and, thanks to them, his butt, running around his head for the rest of the evening.

CHAPTER 5

BRI SAT behind the wheel of his car in the damned parking lot berating himself for being such a damned coward. The guys were right—he *had* been about ready to kiss Obie, but had backed off out of fear. What if one of the guys on the team saw him? What if Obie hadn't wanted him to? Bri had invited Obie to the game as a friend, and he had intended for things to remain that way. And they had in the end, but partway through the game, Bri had found watching Obie much more fascinating than the play on the court. He was an all-in kind of guy. When Obie was excited, he was out of his seat, pumping his arms, bouncing on his feet. A successful basket was an excuse for unbridled joy. It had been a long time since he'd felt that way—about anything. Bri loved his job. He got paid to play the game he'd enjoyed for most of his life, but over time things had become ordinary. Baskets were a means to an end, rather than a joy to make each and every time. His head was on passing and moving the ball, getting past opposing players, throwing them off—not just *playing* and having fun. Tonight, he'd watched Obie and remembered why he'd chosen to play ball for a living. Obie's energy had been infectious.

"Shit." Bri leaned his head on the steering wheel. He wanted that kind of energy in his life.

He jumped at a tap on the window. Catching his breath, he lowered it. "Hey, Ron," he said to one of his teammates who'd come up to his car and was looking in at him in concern.

"You okay? The lot is emptying, and I saw you just sitting there." Ron leaned down with a smile. "The knee doing okay?"

"Yeah. It gets sore sometimes, but I'm healing. I'll be ready for the start of the preseason in a few months. Working hard to get it strong again."

Ron nodded and backed away. "That's good to hear. Good to hear. We're all rooting for you." Ron's expression told him everything. The team, the fans—everyone was behind him, and he needed to come back as strong as he'd been before he got hurt, so he didn't let everyone down. That meant he had to get his head in the game. He couldn't let it wander—no matter how cute a certain therapist was, or how amazing he looked in those damned tight jeans. "You have a good night and let us know if there's anything we can do," Ron added. "You know we're on your side."

He half saluted, and Bri started the car, waving as he pulled out of the lot. He got partway home before the words Ron had used sank into his head. They were on his side… about what? It probably didn't mean anything. But it got him wondering.

Bri instructed the car to dial the phone. "Hey, Dad," he said when his father answered.

"How was the game?" his dad asked. He was probably in bed reading and would be for hours yet. "I hope you had fun with your friends."

"I did. It was fun. I invited Obie, the physical therapist I told you about. He had a great time and even made his free throw shot and won an autographed ball." Bri couldn't help smiling as he slipped into freeway traffic. There was nothing fun about the Schuylkill, but thinking about Obie did that to him.

"That's pretty cool," his dad said, and Bri heard him shuffling around a little.

"He gave the ball to one of the kids," Bri said, and waited for his father's assessment. His dad had spent most of the last forty years or so as a psychology professor at St. Joseph's, and Bri knew everything went through his human-reaction computational brain. He couldn't wait to hear what his dad thought of Obie's behavior.

"He sounds like a person you'll want to stay friends with—" He could almost see his dad smiling at the other end of the line. "—unless he did it for attention."

"No. He just wanted to make a little girl happy. Besides, I can get Obie as many signed balls as he wants. It was a truly kind act."

He braked as the taillights ahead of him lit up. "He was embarrassed about it. The whole thing was caught on the JumboTron, and he tried to hide when he saw it."

"He sounds like the kind of person who isn't going to take advantage of you. At least I'd give him the benefit of the doubt in that department. Who were your other friends?"

"A couple of guys I met with Obie the other night. They're a little out there, but harmless enough. They don't want anything from anyone except a good time." Bri chuckled. "They're all unabashedly gay, Dad. As in, out there unapologetically, makeup-and-glitter-wearing gay." He'd told his father about his own feelings many years earlier. In fact, Bri's habit of keeping quiet about his sexuality had been the subject of a number of conversations between him and his father. He had to give his dad a lot of credit—he could have tried to impose his own ideas on Bri, but he never did.

"You know my feelings on being true to yourself, and I think it's a good idea to have friends that you can talk with about that part of your life." Bri continued the stop-and-go in traffic, nodding his agreement but not interrupting. "As for what others will think, my suggestion is to tell them to go screw themselves." Bri loved his dad.

Bri sighed. "The thing is… I've been getting these phone calls. They're cranks, but the caller keeps telling me that I'm a disgrace to the game and things like that. The first couple I shrugged off, but I'm getting them more and more often. I got one yesterday and then another today." He jammed on the brakes as the car ahead of him came to a sudden stop. "I'm starting to get concerned."

"It sounds like something you should be taking seriously. Come over for lunch tomorrow. Renelda is making her famous carbonara, and you can tell me what's going on." His dad sounded as though he was wearing out for the night, and Bri didn't want to keep him up if he truly thought he could sleep. His dad suffered from severe insomnia, so sleep was a rare commodity sometimes. "Bring this friend of yours, if he'd like to come. It would be nice to talk with someone new." He ended the call, and Bri reached his exit and turned off the freeway, heading out across city streets to his house, pulling into the garage.

He fumbled with his crutches a little, but got out of the car and into the house, locking everything up as he went. His phone chimed as he closed and locked the back door of the early twentieth-century house. *Thank you for a great night. It was amazing. See you soon.*

You're welcome, Obie, he typed and held his fingers over the keyboard of the phone. *I'm going to have lunch with my parents tomorrow. Want to come?* He looked at the message more than once and nearly deleted the last part three times before closing his eyes and pressing Send. He watched the screen for a response, and when one didn't come immediately, he figured Obie was trying to think of a way to turn him down.

Sounds like fun. What should I bring?

He let out a sigh of relief.

I'll pick you up at eleven thirty. Dad loves dessert, but doesn't get it very often. He sent the message, and Obie responded with a smiley face, which he took to mean everything was good to go. His knee ached and he'd already spent enough time on it, so he labored up the stairs, going right to the master bath and running a tub of water. After getting undressed and out of the brace, he sighed as he carefully lowered himself in the tub and turned on the whirlpool jets. Now that was heaven—at least until the water cooled.

BRI CHECKED the time—again—late the following morning, before leaving to head to Obie's. The drive on a Sunday morning was very easy, and he pulled around back to his usual place, where Obie was waiting for him with a plasticware cake container. "Don't tell me you baked that yourself?"

"It's a chocolate pie, and I already had the shell, so I just made the rest." He smiled as he got in, balancing the container on his lap. "I hope it's something your dad will like. You didn't give me much to go on last night."

"Dad adores chocolate. Mom and Renelda are probably going to pitch a fit, but that's fine. It's good for them and for Dad to get some of what he doesn't have often." Bri backed out of the space and headed west, along the main line to the house in Bala Cynwyd.

"Who's Renelda?" Obie asked.

"She's... well, it's hard to say exactly. She's my mother housekeeper and has been with the family for years. She also helps take care of my dad. He has ALS, so he's confined to a wheelchair and, unfortunately, has less and less physical mobility each year. He says it's like being slowly sunk in quicksand and never being able to get out. His mind is still as sharp as always, though. He's a highly regarded professor and used to get asked to travel all over the country as a guest lecturer and speaker."

"I see. And your mother?"

"The power behind the throne, if you will. She and Renelda have done wonders to keep Dad comfortable and as healthy as possible. He's still able to work a fairly full schedule, but that's because they handle the everyday things so he can do what he truly loves." He pulled to a stop and looked over at Obie. "I hope I haven't scared you off."

"Why would you think that?"

"Dad is...." Bri paused a second. "He's always assessing people, and sometimes he can be incredibly intimidating. When I was growing up, a lot of my friends were scared to meet him. They were afraid he could read their minds or something. But Dad asked to meet you. In fact, it was his suggestion that I invite you to come with me."

Obie sat back, his hands clutching the container. "So... is this some kind of test or something?"

"God, no." Bri had to do a little backpedaling. "I was talking to him last night after the game and I told him about you. He said he wanted to meet you and asked if I'd invite you to come along. Dad finds people who do the unexpected interesting. And the whole thing last night with the basketball was definitely unexpected. Just be yourself."

"That's easy for you to say," Obie said.

"Don't worry. The chocolate pie will go a long way in winning him over." Bri smiled.

"And it will piss off your mother at the same time." Obie huffed.

Bri chuckled. "Nope. Mom adores chocolate. Just ignore the way she chastises my father for wanting a large piece, because she'll be in seventh heaven herself." Bri winked. "Believe me, it's a great choice." He turned off the road and onto a long circular driveway up to a Tudor-style house with a manicured lawn and neat formal hedges.

"This is stunning. Who is the gardener in the family?"

"My dad. He designed and planted the entire property when I was a kid. Mom now uses a garden service to keep it just the way Dad likes it. Whenever they show up, he rolls out in his chair and tells them exactly what he wants done. It's his passion, and I know he wishes he could get down on the ground and dig in the dirt again." More than anything, Bri wished his dad could do that too.

"Has your father lost any movement in his hands and arms?" Obie asked with what sounded to Bri like genuine concern.

"Some. He can't do incredibly detailed work, but he still types, albeit slowly. Why?"

"You could have someone make your dad some raised beds that are the same height as his chair. Then he could wheel himself next to them and plant and care for the gardens himself. They don't need to be big. In fact, you could make them about four feet long, but only a foot wide. He could fill them with flowers or vegetables. Whatever he wanted." Obie turned to him, and Bri felt his chin nearly hit the steering wheel as he pulled to a stop. Why in the hell hadn't he thought of that?

"Now I know what I'm going to get him for Father's Day. I could make them portable, so they could be moved once he was done and placed where he can water and care for them." Without thinking, Bri took Obie's hand, squeezing it. "That is an amazing idea."

"Part of what I do is physical therapy, but I also do occupational therapy, or at least I used to at the drive-through clinic."

"What's the difference?" Bri asked. He'd heard the words, but had never given them much thought.

"Physical therapy is what you and I are doing. The purpose is to help you heal and get back into peak physical condition. Occupational therapy is what they did when they taught you how to use crutches or when they showed you how to put your shoes and socks on without reinjuring yourself. It's to show you how to navigate life again after the injury. In your dad's case, the flower boxes would help him get back something he's lost, in a different way. But it could also help with his motion and delay further loss. Use it or lose it."

"Is that real?" Bri put the car in Park and turned to Obie, grinning as his mind whirred on what he could do for his dad. Dammit, he knew he was beaming, but couldn't help it.

"Yes. If we didn't work your leg every week like we are, you might improve, but your muscles could heal in such a way that you might not get all the motion back. Or it could heal badly and get worse over time. It's hard to push ourselves each and every day unless we have some goal or something we love that makes us want to do it." Obie shrugged. "I'm glad you like the idea. It was just a thought off the top of my head." Bri didn't move, and Obie continued looking at him. Bri felt heat building, and not from the sun shining in the windows.

Damn it all, Bri wanted to know what those pink, slightly pursed lips tasted like and what it would feel like to kiss Obie, to pull that compact, wiry body to him. Was Obie the electric spark he thought he was? He had to know. So he leaned across the console to get closer, using the excuse of looking into the glove compartment as a chance to inhale Obie's enticingly rich scent, which only made matters more difficult and... problematic.

"Are you coming in or do you plan to sit in your car all day?" His mother stood outside, hands on her hips. Instantly, things cooled down for him, even if a little sweat broke out on the back of his neck. Bri opened the door and carefully got out, getting his crutches from the back seat. Obie came around to meet him once he got his crutches under his arms.

"Mom, this is Obie," Bri said.

"The friend your father was taking about," she said, extending her hand. Obie shifted the container and shook the offered hand.

"It's a pleasure to meet you." It was clear that Obie wasn't sure what to do with the container.

Bri helped him out. "Obie made Dad a chocolate dessert." He knew his mother was too well-mannered to actually say anything about it in front of him. She took the container and motioned toward the house.

"Porter will love it, I'm sure." She smiled and led them inside. Obie stayed with him and let Bri enter first. His mother headed toward the kitchen, and Bri led Obie into the living room, where his father sat in his chair near the front window.

"You must be Obie. Bri was telling me about you last night." He waved toward a nearby chair, and Obie sat down. "So tell me why you gave away your basketball."

Obie glanced at him, and Bri shrugged. "Dad, you could beat around the bush a little."

"Poppycock. Take them by surprise." He leaned closer to Obie. "So why did you do it?"

"Dad…," Bri groaned.

"It's okay. I love basketball, always have. But I was too short, so they didn't want me on the team until they learned I could shoot. Anyway, I made the shot, and when I went to take my seat, I saw a little girl a few rows up. She had this look on her face—you know the one, like she wanted something more than anything else in the world. So I gave her the ball. I think it will mean more to her than it ever would to me."

Porter shook his head. "I have seen very few true acts of kindness in my life. We often do things for selfish reasons—because we want something in return, even if it's recognition."

"It never occurred to me," Obie said with a shrug. "There was no thought behind it. It was spontaneous." Obie blushed slightly. "Can we talk about something else?"

Bri was about to say the same thing, but he knew his dad, and he wasn't likely to let this go yet. He could almost see the questions bubbling up in his eyes. "Yes, Dad."

His dad huffed. "Very well." He slowly turned to Obie. "I didn't mean to make you uncomfortable." That was unusual. By and large, his father's entire career had been built around making people uncomfortable as he tried to get them to examine the source of their feelings, which tended to be traumatic. "I encounter someone truly kind very seldom and I was curious."

Obie cocked his head slowly, and his lips curled upward just a little. "Okay. As long as you're willing to answer my questions, I'll answer yours."

"Agreed." Bri's dad smiled and a light grew in his eyes. "Did you consider that she might not want the ball? To be closed-minded and stereotypical, it *was* a little girl that you gave the ball to, not a little boy, right?"

Obie grinned. "She was there with her dad, so it never occurred to me. I gave it to her because I thought it would make her happy." He leaned forward. "So, my turn. Why did you name your son Brighton Early? Did you not consider the implications of that kind of name on him? Did you, as an educator, not consider how other people would treat him because of it?"

Bri nearly gasped. Not that he was shocked by the question, but because he had never thought to ask his dad about it. He had gone by a nickname since he was six years old. He didn't like his name and had spent much of his life distancing himself from it. "Obie...."

Porter snickered, a sound he had very rarely heard his dad ever make. "That is one of the best questions anyone has ever asked me. I named my son Brighton because I liked the name. Pamela and I did think about it briefly, but we figured it would either make him stronger or help him figure out who he was and what he wanted." His dad's smile faded. "I had no idea that he would spend the rest of his life stepping back from his own name."

"You know that names matter," Obie said. "They're important. They label you and help others identify you. They give an impression of you before you even open your mouth." He raised his eyebrows, challenging Porter, which happened very rarely. It was a little satisfying for Bri to see his father put off his game, even if just a little.

"I see. I take it this is something you feel strongly about." Porter locked gazes with Obie. "Do you have an unusual name?" Bri had seen his father's laser focus more times in his life than he could count. Obie swallowed, his throat working as he nodded.

"Dad…," Bri groaned a warning,

"He asked his question, so I get to ask mine." To his father, that would seem logical.

"Yes. My father has a weird sense of humor. Obediah Juan Kenoble," Obie said, and Bri's father gasped. "They're family names."

"Okay. Son, I owe you an apology," he said as he turned to Bri. "We should have been more sensitive to the potential impacts of naming you Brighton Early. I thought I was giving you something that would make you stronger, not a millstone that you had to carry around with you for your entire life." He held out his hand, and Bri took it.

"Dad, I'm Bri. That's the name I take for my own, the same way I take and own the rest of the things in my life that are important to me. I know who I am." His father rarely apologized directly. Not that he didn't say he was sorry, but he usually did it with actions rather than saying it directly.

"Boys, we're getting lunch on the table." His mom came in and leaned down, kissing his dad gently. "You be nice to Obie. He brought you a chocolate dessert. And you know Renelda and I are not going make you dessert."

"We're good, dear. He and I were having a wonderful conversation." Porter smiled. "I like him."

Bri and Obie shared a glance, and Bri nodded. His dad never said things he didn't mean. "Mom, I'll help Dad get in for lunch," Bri offered, and his mother thanked him and left the room. He stood, then guided his father away from the desk and out into the open so he could easily navigate out of the living room and into the dining area.

He turned to Obie. "Dad and mom don't have many guests at mealtime," Bri said.

"I suspect your dad is self-conscious when he eats." Obie patted his arm. "Come on, let's go in. The lunch smells amazing." While Bri's dad had movement in his arms and hands, it could be jerky, which meant that sometimes the food didn't make it to his mouth. They entered the dining room, and Bri moved his dad to where he sat at the end of the table. Places had been set for Bri and Obie along one side, with his mother across from them. Renelda brought in the food and then took a place next to Bri's mother.

"Thank you for having me," Obie said a little nervously.

"I'm only glad I haven't scared you away already. I spent too many years getting into other people's heads to turn it off that easily. Pamela tells me over and over that I need to lay off and just let it go."

"Turning off part of who you are is an exercise in futility," Obie said, with both Bri's father and mother nodding their heads. Bri couldn't agree more.

BRI SPENT most of lunch as tense as a banjo string. It wasn't because things weren't going well. They were, in fact, going great, but he kept expecting the situation to go off the rails at any time. Especially after Bri's father finished eating and started scanning around the table. Oh God, Dad was thinking of his next questions. But none came.

"Mr. Brighton, how is your knee?" Renelda asked as she began clearing the dishes and bringing coffee. She always called him that, no matter how many times he asked her to stop. It was her way of showing him respect.

"It's doing better, thank you. Obie is helping me get back into playing form. We've already been seeing progress, which is making me very happy."

She nodded and smiled.

"Have you thought about what you want to do with your life after basketball?" his dad interrupted. "You know your mother and I support you—we always have and we always will—but this injury should be a wake-up call that your career has a shelf life." His dad seldom asked easy questions, and he must have been saving this one up for a while.

"I don't know," Bri answered and looked at both his parents. "Right now, I want to focus on getting back into playing form and then concentrate on playing my best."

"It's what Bri and I are working on." Obie picked up for him. "If all my clients were as cautious and took their recovery as seriously as he does, my job would be a lot easier. He's driven to recover. That goes a long way in getting him back to where he should be." Obie squeezed his hand under the table.

"Isn't that being shortsighted?" Bri's father pressed.

Bri opened his mouth, but didn't get a chance to answer before Obie jumped in to defend him. "Being an athlete takes a huge amount of dedication." Obie leaned forward, tilting his head to Bri's dad. "I think it's important that we all keep our eye on the ball and where it belongs." Obie turned to him. "Personally, I'd love to see Bri as a model. I think he'd be fantastic in one of those underwear ads." He fanned himself slightly.

Bri's mom giggled. "I'd like to see that too, as long as he wears clothes. The last thing I want to see is a forty-foot-tall poster of my baby boy wearing nothing but a pair of Calvin Klein tighty-whities. I don't think any mother wants to see that." She shivered and Bri nearly choked on his drink. Obie turned to him with heat in his eyes. Obviously, Obie had a very different opinion from his mom, and Bri found he liked that Obie found that intriguing.

"But what about a real career?" his father asked without heat, though obviously trying to get the topic back where he wanted it. "You'll need to make a living when you can't play any longer."

Renelda finished clearing the table, and Bri figured she was smart to get out of the line of fire. He and his dad had had this discussion before, but his injury had only strengthened his dad's argument. "Dad, right now, I want to continue playing. That's where I need to put my energy."

"You have a college degree. Maybe now is a good time to use your contacts to check out some other opportunities. What if your knee never heals enough that you can play again?" The firmness in his dad's voice caught Bri a little off guard.

"What did you study?" Obie asked gently from next to him.

"I took business classes. I could go on for an MBA if I wanted, at some point. But I love what I do, and the thought of hours in classrooms again, followed by days in an office, makes my skin crawl." He turned to his dad. "You always did your best for us, but I don't want your life. The thought of living like that makes me stir-crazy."

He firmed his tone to meet the one his dad had used. "What I want is an active life." He turned to Obie, because if he continued staring at his dad—and seeing the way he glared at him—Bri was going to say something he didn't mean. And the last thing he wanted was a full-on fight in front of Obie. "I've been thinking of working with kids." He grinned. "I have this idea of starting a camp, maybe closer to the city. I could work with people who are as passionate about basketball as I am—teach them some of what I've learned and maybe help them discover that they have a talent they never knew about."

His dad shook his head, but he was smiling, which was confusing as all fuck. "You look like you have something to say?" Bri said to his dad.

"Yes. I think that's a great idea." His dad actually seemed pleased. "Son, I don't care what you do as long as it makes you happy. But if you want something like that to happen, you need to start thinking about it now." He yawned, and his mother helped wipe his father's face and clean up his clothes.

"Go into the living room. I'll help Renelda here and will join you in a few minutes." She effectively kicked them out of the dining room, and Bri couldn't help noticing the amount of food scattered on the table around his dad's plate. He sighed and said nothing, even though he knew it was a sign of the progression of his dad's disease. But he noticed the way Obie looked at the table, also saying nothing.

"The meal was lovely, thank you," Obie said, flashing both Bri's mom and Renelda one of his winning smiles, which Bri instantly wished had been aimed his way.

"The powder room is just down the hall if you need to refresh yourself." His mother was always big on her guests being refreshed. He used to laugh at the term until he realized how much better it sounded than the alternative.

"Thank you." Obie went down the hall, and Bri followed him.

"Dad's getting worse," Bri said softly, hoping that if he said something, it might ease the twist in his gut. "He could eat much more easily a few months ago." He leaned against the wall of the hallway, where family pictures filled almost every inch of space.

Obie nodded and blessedly didn't offer some platitude to try to make him feel better.

"I'm not sure what to do." Bri kept his voice low.

Obie shrugged. "Be there for him?" he offered. Bri nodded as the back of his throat scratched. He swallowed, hoping it would go away, but that wasn't likely. His father's condition was only going to get worse… until it killed him. He swallowed again and turned away. "Is that you?" Bri turned to the picture Obie was looking at.

"No. My brother. He loved horses and rode competitively when he was younger. Mom and Dad had joined the country club, where they had stables. He won a number of ribbons. That's his first one, with Dancer. Mom and Dad got him for us to share, but Dancer bonded with him. They were inseparable, and Gregory used to go out to the barn every single day to care for him and ride him."

Obie stared at the picture of Gregory standing next to Dancer, holding his ribbon, one hand caressing Dancer's neck. "There's a story there."

Bri nodded. "I wish I could say it was a happy one. Someone broke into the stable one night, and Dancer got out. By the time we found him, he'd hurt his leg so badly that there was no hope for him. We'd had him five years at that point, so Gregory was heartbroken." Bri moved down the hall. "This is the two of them a few weeks before the incident."

"They look great together." Obie stared at the picture.

"Yeah, they did. Dad offered to get Gregory another horse, but he declined. As far as I know, he has never ridden again. He had no interest in it after we lost Dancer."

"What does he do now?" Obie smiled as he slid his gaze down the rest of the walls of pictures. "Is that him?" He pointed to a picture of Bri's brother at his college graduation, complete with cap, gown, and honors insignia.

"Gregory went into special education. He always had this huge heart." Bri sighed. "Gregory is the best of all of us. He originally wanted to be an architect and used to dream of designing buildings that would last forever. But that changed his sophomore year." He motioned to the next picture. "That's Gregory and Phillip. He joined Big Brothers, and when he met Phillip...." Bri swallowed hard. "Phillip had special needs, and no one wanted to take him. Gregory didn't bat an eyelash. He spent a lot of time with him for the next three years, until Phillip's heart just gave out." Dammit, he had to turn away and tried to wipe his eyes so Obie wouldn't see.

A hand, warm and gentle, rested on his shoulder and stayed there. Thankfully, Obie knew when to remain quiet. If he'd said one word, Bri would have lost it.

"Gregory stayed in school another year, changed his major, and went into education. Dad was thrilled that his oldest son was following in his footsteps, so to speak. Gregory taught in the classroom for a number of years and developed programs to help kids like Phillip and others. His work has been published, and two years ago, he was promoted to principal. The kids love him." He took a deep breath, noticing that Obie's hand didn't leave his shoulder.

"You know that isn't necessarily true." He met Obie's gaze, wondering what he was getting at. "You have a big heart too, you know."

Bri sighed as Obie glanced each way and then slid closer as Bri shifted fully around to face him. Obie's hand slid upward along his neck, and he came close enough that Obie's scent curled through his nose. He stiffened, his gaze latching on to Obie's, his heart racing a little faster with each passing second. Was this really going to happen?

He thought for a fraction of a second, leaning closer until Obie's lips met his.

The touch was whisper light for a millisecond. Then Obie leaned in, adding pressure as sparks flew between them. He gasped slightly at the intensity, and Obie backed away. Bri wound his arms around Obie's slender waist, tugging him close once again, this time pressing him to the wall so he couldn't get away as he got the full taste of him. Peaches and cream, ambrosia, chocolate—all paled in comparison to the sweet heat that radiated off Obie and slid right across Bri's tongue. He wanted more, his body screamed for it, and before he could stop himself, his hips rocked slightly because his jeans were suddenly way too damn tight.

Bri tensed as a throat cleared behind him, and he held Obie tighter, putting his body between Obie and whoever was behind him. He pulled away and turned, blushing in the light of his mother's amused expression. "When you two are done, your father has asked for you." She cocked her eyebrows the same way she had when he was twelve and had been caught sneaking back into the house after having spent the night in Jenny Wilson's backyard telling ghost stories.

"I was just telling Obie about Gregory and Dancer." He needed to say something, and he'd be damned if he was going to apologize— not for a kiss that was worth waiting an entire lifetime for.

"I can see that." She turned back down the hall, and Obie blushed as red as the graduation gown in Gregory's picture.

"Caught by your mother," he whispered.

Bri smiled and tried kissing the embarrassment away. "That's not the worst thing my mother has caught me doing." He leaned closer. "I discovered the bathroom lock was broken once… the hard way, if you know what I mean."

Obie sputtered and flushed even more. "I once walked in on my mom and dad… in the bedroom… in the middle of things."

Damn, he loved that Obie could blush like that.

Bri shrugged. "What kid hasn't?"

Obie shook his head. "It's a real interesting way to find out just how kinky your mom and dad truly are." He grinned and then laughed.

"It seems that my mother and father have a thing for leather." He rolled his eyes. "There are some things in my life I really wish I could unsee, and Mom in a leather brassiere and Dad in chaps—and nothing else—is definitely one of them."

It took a second for the image to register before Bri covered his mouth. "Okay, you win." He took Obie's hand, smiling that he could do that now, and led Obie through the house to where his dad was watching television. He turned it off when they came in, and Bri sat down with Obie next to him.

"I think we need to talk about these messages you've been getting," his dad said, sliding his chair nearer.

"What messages?" Obie asked.

Bri pulled out his phone and played the messages. "The sender is always blocked, and when I try to trace the numbers back, I get nowhere, so I think they're being masked."

"Do you recognize the voice?" Obie listened. "What about that Donald guy? He was being pretty threatening the other day, the skank." Obie didn't hold things back, that was for sure.

"It isn't him, or at least it's not his voice. That doesn't mean he isn't behind it, though." Bri played the first message again and turned to his dad for some insight.

"What does he mean when he says you ignored the message? How long have you been getting these calls?"

"The first articulated threat was about ten days ago," Bri answered.

"I was wondering about that too," Obie said. "Did you get something in the mail or at work? Was anything sent to the team?"

Bri shook his head.

"I don't think it's that kind of message," his dad mused. "It's more likely something that happened, something meant to have meaning, only Bri didn't recognize it. But what? Play the messages again." He did, but Bri was becoming tired of this man's voice and the cryptic way he spoke.

"Who else doesn't like that you might be gay?" Obie asked. That seemed to be a point of contention for this guy.

"That seems to be the trigger. But your preferences aren't widely known, are they?" his dad asked, and Bri shook his head.

"I got one after visiting the club. I was there to help drum up support for AIDS research. Still, anyone could have seen me go in and made assumptions. But there were plenty of people there who came to help out. That didn't mean that everyone there was gay," Bri reasoned.

"I don't think that's the point. This guy is obsessed with you and who you're seeing and where you're going. And he isn't happy." His dad seemed to be thinking. "Play them all one last time…. Stop." His dad paused. "Right there. That reference to knowing what you've done. It's like you've hurt this person, or they think that you've done something to them." He closed his eyes. "Perceived hurts can be just as damaging and hurtful as real ones."

"But what could I have done? I don't…." He was at a loss. "This whole thing is starting to freak me out. At first I thought it was just a crank call and didn't pay it any attention."

His dad's eyes bored into him. "You have to take this seriously. You don't know what this person is capable of, and I don't want you to find out. Send me the messages, and I'll give it some thought. Maybe there's something in them that I haven't considered."

Bri agreed and set about sending the messages to his dad, as his mom and Renelda brought in slices of Obie's chocolate dessert. They all settled in to eat, and thankfully the conversation shifted to lighter topics.

TOO STUPID for words! That's what I am! And this fucking room is way too small. I need to get the hell out of here. I've spent too much time talking. Talk is fucking cheap! I stare at the phone in my hand. Clenching it tightly, my arms shake in rage. It has failed me. The time for action has arrived, and this time, I'm taking matters into my own hands.

CHAPTER 6

HEARING THOSE messages scared Obie to death. He agreed with Porter that Bri had to take the threat seriously. "Your dad is a pretty interesting guy." As they rode home, Obie couldn't help dwelling on the afternoon's conversation. "You know, I'm sorry if this guy is after you because of me."

"You?"

"Well, you got one after being with me at the club and then after we ran into Donald." He really thought that jerk was behind this, but wasn't sure how to prove it.

"I don't think you have anything to do with it." Obie wished that was true, but somehow, he doubted it. "I keep going back to who was at the club," Bri continued. "There were plenty of people around. It could be anyone. Then again, given the club's clientele, I'd think most of the people there would be supportive and not angry if I came out."

Obie hummed as he thought. "The messages keep repeating that you're a disgrace to the sport. But what if this doesn't have anything to do with you being gay? What if it has something to do with your play? It's well known that you're aggressive and that you will do almost anything to make a basket. This could be some superfan—one who's a little off his rocker—from another team who's angry with you." Obie kept running through scenarios in his head, but they all ended up at the same place, which wasn't helping.

"Let's talk about something else." Bri flashed him a bright smile. "Like getting a cup of coffee."

"Been through the wringer?" It was a little hard not to be slightly amused.

"Yeah." Bri sighed as he continued driving. "I need to go home and get my leg up for a while." He continued driving past Obie's exit, and Obie sat back in the plush seat. He didn't have any plans for the rest of the day. "What were you going to do this afternoon?"

"Laundry," Obie answered with a soft chuckle. "I lead such a wild social life."

"What about the guys?" Bri asked. "I sort of thought you spent a lot of time together."

"They're my best friends and I see them a few times a week, but I like to think I have a life of my own, boring as it is." He smiled and closed his eyes. "I was more than a little nervous about meeting your parents. I like your mom. My guess is that she can be a real hardass, but she's one heck of a hostess. And your dad, what a hoot." Obie had liked both of them immensely, especially Porter. He was an interestingly forceful man.

"Dad liked you. It isn't often that someone can go toe to toe with him." Bri made the turnoff and continued to his house, pulling into the driveway.

"I'm surprised you don't have security. With the threats you've been getting, maybe it's something you should think about." Obie didn't want to tell Bri what to do, but given his profession, living alone without some protection… it just seemed a little risky.

"I have a security system that I engage whether I'm home or away. I don't really have much that's worth stealing. You can see that Mom and Dad don't live cluttered lives, so I never did either. I'd rather spend my money on travel and preparing for a life after basketball than splurging on fancy furniture and stuff." Bri pulled into the garage, and Obie got out of the car, going around in case Bri needed help. He seemed to be managing well on his own, though, and Obie followed him inside.

The house was of moderate size, clean, and sparsely furnished. The living room had leather sofas with a bright geometric rug on the floor in front of a massive television. There were a few lamps and pictures on the walls, probably courtesy of Pamela. Obie stood near Bri and made sure there was room for him to stretch out. "I can make the coffee if you tell me where it is in the kitchen. You put your leg up and rest it. I hear you have a therapy session on Tuesday and the therapist is a real badass."

"Tell me about it," Bri teased, and Obie followed his directions, finding the coffee pods and putting them in the Keurig, then returning with two mugs of coffee and setting them on the glass coffee table. He sat down, watching Bri, wondering what could possibly be going on in his head, and thinking about the kiss in his parents' hallway.

"I'm sorry about earlier," Bri finally said. "I probably should have asked… or something, before I…." Obie stood and closed the distance between them, locking gazes with Bri.

"What exactly are you sorry for?" Obie didn't look away or blink, keeping Bri in his sights. "You should be specific." He leaned down, a hand on the armrest. "Was it this?" Obie asked as he kissed Bri, deepening it as he slipped his hand around the back of his neck, just as he'd done before. Bri's eyes had glassed over slightly by the time he pulled back. "Or maybe it was this…." He brought their lips together again, straddling Bri, being careful of his leg, but letting him know that a little making out was not unwanted. "Was that it?"

Bri's pupils had widened to saucers, and he nodded and half shook his head at the same time, as if he wasn't too damned certain of very much at the moment. "I'm not sure. It seemed like the proper thing to say."

"Okay. Let me let you in on a secret. When you kiss someone hard enough and with enough energy to curl their toes and take their breath away, you don't apologize for it. You thank God for each and every second, and then do it again." He raised his eyebrows, and Bri nodded, tugging him closer, strong arms encircling his waist. God, it was heady as hell being held like this, and when Bri's lips took his this time, Obie added his own energy, feeding off Bri's and sending it back until his head reeled and thinking became a chore. Not that it mattered. Thinking was fucking overrated. And all Obie cared about at the moment was how easily he could coax Bri off the sofa and up into his bedroom to see if sex with this intense man was as good as being kissed by him.

Instead, Obie pulled away, the passion that clouded his head fading just a little. He stood on wobbly legs, flopping down into the nearby chair and reaching for the coffee. "I think I need this to cool down." Holy hell, what he needed was a cold shower that lasted for a month. Bri was a client, someone he worked with, and getting involved with him was unethical.

"Obie...," Bri said, his tone resonant, settling at the base of Obie's balls.

"Look, I'm your therapist, and...." He took a deep breath, releasing, concentrating on his breathing, hoping to clear his head, somehow. "We can't do this. I need to be able to work with you as a client, so you can play again. You know that, I know that." He sat back, wondering what kind of idiot he truly was. "I can't do that if my head is wondering what your lips taste like or what you feel like under that shirt." His belly did a little loop. "I think we need to take a step back so we can remember what the goal is." He had to think about that a little himself. Obie forced himself to move away, trying not to let the disappointment in Bri's eyes influence him. But damn, that was a lot harder than it should have been.

"You're really going to hide behind that kind of old-fashioned thinking?" Bri countered.

Obie put his hands on his hips. "I have a professional reputation, and I'm good at what I do. But if word got around that I slept with my clients, then suddenly I'd have a ton of them thinking I was some kind of gigolo. I can't have that." He watched Bri's eyes as the idea registered. "I think you can understand that."

Bri nodded. "I can, and I don't want to hurt you." That was the truth; Obie heard it ring in Bri's voice. But the longing in his eyes was palpable, mesmerizing, and made Obie want to chuck all his good intentions.

"Then we need to take things slowly. And the first part of that is to get you back on your feet. Once you're no longer my client, we can talk about taking things in a different direction." Go him. That was the sensible thing to do, and he needed to stick with it.

"I could just look for another therapist," Bri offered.

Obie hardened his lips. "Is that what you really want to do? Put your recovery in jeopardy because you want to take me to bed?" He refused to believe that.

"Are you saying you aren't worth it?" Bri countered.

Obie grinned slyly. "Oh, I know I am. You'd better believe it. But I can't let that happen. If your goal is to continue playing, then we need to keep that first and foremost. Let's get you well and keep the rest on the back burner. You are going to have enough challenges over the next few weeks without added complications." He took a deep breath. "We both know that I'm the best one to help you regain your playing form, so let's do that." He leaned closer in the chair. "Besides, if things turned out badly, I'd never forgive myself. You'd come to resent me and you know it."

Bri twisted his lips slightly.

"You know I'm right, whether you want to admit it or not." Obie sometimes hated to be right, and this was one of those times. "So we can be friends, but we have to keep the rest at arm's length." It was going to be hard enough massaging Bri's legs without thinking of the hardness that had pressed against him earlier, without daydreaming about how firm and strong Bri was. The man pushed all his buttons.

"You're right. I know that." Bri's expression didn't lessen, but it cooled somewhat, and he leaned over the table to pick up his mug of coffee.

"There's more at stake here than just my professional reputation. There's yours as well." Obie hated to bring this up, but knew it had to be said. "You know I'm not in the closet in any way, but you still are. Everyone thinks Bri Early is settled and secure in his sexuality. But they don't know the real you." Obie sniffed because he couldn't believe he was about to say what he had to.

"Is this about Donald?" Bri asked.

"In a way. What do you think the rest of your team will say when they find out you're dating another guy? That you're dating someone like me? We were just at the game last night and some asshole gave me shit. Do you want to be on the receiving end of that kind of crap? Because it will come. Not everyone is going to accept you. I wish they would, but they won't. There are plenty of assholes in this world." Obie figured he'd said enough to throw cold water on Bri's ardor.

"You're saying I should keep quiet until I retire? Others have given me the same advice. But I didn't think I'd get that from…."

Obie sighed. "Someone like me," he added, finishing the sentence he knew was coming. "Because I'm a little twinkie and like to wear makeup and nice clothes, I should be marching in pride parades and screaming to everyone to come out of the closet." He set his mug down. "Maybe that is what I think, but this isn't about me. This is about you and what's best so you can do what you love— at least until you truly can't do it any longer." Listen to him be all unselfish and shit. But it was the right thing to say, even if it hurt to say the words. "Do what's best for you and what you want. What everyone else thinks or says is bullshit. And that includes me."

"I'm a good player. The team isn't going to cut me loose for being gay," Bri argued.

"Probably not," Obie agreed. "But what if your teammates stop guarding you or stop passing to you? It would be easy enough for them to cut you out. The team will suffer, sure… but in the end they'll remove the single point of failure rather than changing the whole team. That's just good business." He softened his posture. "And what if someone hurts you? Are you prepared for that? You got injured in an exhibition game that was supposed to be just a friendly match, and the guy who did it…." Obie grew silent as a notion took hold, running like ice water down his back.

"What?" Bri asked. "Why are you as white as a ghost?"

"We need to get the video of that game, and take a look at the part when you were injured." He hated to even say it, but the notion wasn't going to go away now that the seed had been planted in his mind. "What if your injury was the message you were supposed to have understood?"

"Huh?" Bri rolled his eyes. "You have to be kidding. It was an accident. Things like that can happen during games. Don't you think you're jumping to conclusions?"

"Let's get your computer and take a look. There are a number of videos of the accident on YouTube from various people who were there."

Bri groaned. "The laptop is in the office."

Obie ignored his attitude and retrieved it, then sat next to Bri and booted it up. Moments later, they had at least a dozen clips to choose from. Of course, no one was actually supposed to be filming the game, but it was impossible to police everyone. "Check out this one." Obie started the clip. It was from farther up, but it was pretty steady. "Right there."

"What?"

"He came across. Did you see? Young was guarding Williams, and suddenly he was in your face. He ran a quarter of the way across the court to get to you, and when he got close, suddenly you go down with a knee injury." He got another clip, this one closer and from the sidelines. It was difficult to see the exact angle they needed, but it was clear that the opposing player had indeed gone after Bri. Up to that point, he had been staying in position, guarding one of the other players.

"Things get chaotic during a game. These clips don't prove anything. Maybe he saw an opening and thought I was going to go for the ball," Bri reasoned, but Obie wasn't buying it.

"Do you have a grudge with Young? Have you talked to him? Do you think he could be the guy who made the calls?" Obie asked, playing yet another video. "I know what I'm saying sounds a little out there, but what if it's true? What if Young truly intended to injure you?"

"Why?" Bri asked. "I barely know the guy. We've never been on the same team, and he joined the league just two years ago. He's a good player, but I doubt he'll ever be a superstar. Why would he want to hurt me? Yeah, the game had taken on a more serious tone than exhibition play usually did, but to purposely injure someone else…." He blinked and locked gazes with Obie. "Do you really think it's possible?"

"I don't know. This isn't my area of expertise, but I remember seeing the replay of the game and I thought Young's move was completely wrong at the time. Something really bothered me, but it isn't until I look at it now that I think I see why." He ran through all the other clips, but they didn't show much of anything else. "All I'm saying is, what if?" He closed the computer lid and set it on the coffee table. "Maybe I am just plain wrong… or maybe there's something else going on."

"Okay…," Bri agreed reluctantly.

"Why don't you run it by your dad and see what he thinks," Obie offered, and stood up. "I think I should go home. But you need to be careful. Whoever is threatening you could be dangerous. I know you think you're pretty invincible, but you aren't… any more than I am." He didn't want anything to happen to Bri. "I'll see you Tuesday for our appointment." He leaned closer and lightly kissed Bri, because there was no way he was going to leave without one last kiss. "Now take me home."

It was both the longest and shortest ride in history.

OBIE'S HEART beat a little faster Tuesday afternoon as he finished his appointment and got the area set up for Bri. He had planned to start with a massage, but second-guessed himself because touching Bri probably wasn't the best idea. Crap, this was why he was taking a step back. He had to be able to treat Bri without his thoughts immediately going to sex. This was a therapy session, nothing more, and he needed to be professional about it.

Bri came in, and Obie met him at the door. "Are you ready?" His throat went dry as he looked at Bri. His shorts hugged his thick thighs, and Obie turned away, trying not to let his mind go on a wayward journey.

"Yes. My leg has been a little sore, but less so every day." He stood a little taller.

"That's good…."

"Look, Obie, we can stand here and act like there's nothing between us, or we can just be ourselves." Bri smiled, and Obie blew air out from between his lips. "Let's get to work, okay?"

"Sure. Hop up on the table, and we'll start with some massage like we have before and then we'll work your leg." He sighed and waited while Bri took off his shoes and climbed onto the massage table, lying facedown to start with. Obie got to work, loosening the muscles in his leg and trying not to notice Bri's perfect, strong butt or the way his leg muscles flexed and relaxed under his touch.

"Are the exercises getting any easier?"

"Yes, and I think I'm seeing more flexibility." Bri rolled over, and Obie loosened his thighs and lower leg. He wasn't supposed to pay attention to the bulge in Bri's shorts or allow his mouth to go dry. He turned away, forcing his attention where it belonged, and ignored the sheen of sweat that broke out on the back of his neck. Damn, this was going to be more difficult than he figured. Still, he was a professional, and he was going to do the job he was being paid for.

"Good. You're making progress. Now let's go through the exercises and work on your flexibility." He had to do something more active or his head was going to explode.

Obie spent the next half hour working on Bri's legs and knees. The muscles were strengthening and he was regaining flexibility. Obie was still worried, but kept it to himself, that regardless of what they did, there was going to be a part of Bri's mobility that was going to be lost. Hopefully it wouldn't be much, but with this type of injury, 100 percent mobility recovery was rare.

"What aren't you saying?" Bri asked as he lay back on the mat. "You have that look."

Obie sat back on his haunches. "You're making a lot of progress. I can see that. But… I have worries about full range of motion. You have scar tissue, and that is going to impede your mobility long-term." He sighed. "So I want to try some different things this time. We have been working on bending your knee, but we also need to manage body rotation and other movements."

"I'm ready when you are," Bri said gently and sat up, his eyes locking with Obie's. Instantly, heat welled under his clothes. Obie swallowed hard and had to be the first to turn away from the intensity in Bri's gaze. "I want this, Obie," he added in a whisper, and Obie took a second to wonder if he meant playing, him… or both.

"Then let's do it together."

The remainder of the session was a lot of hard work that left Obie drained from trying to keep his head where it belonged and monitoring Bri's physical exertion. By the time he said goodbye and made sure Bri made it to his car and was able to drive away, he needed a drink and a cold shower. Thankfully, he had a couple of days to get his head where it belonged.

Since Bri was his last appointment of the day, he showered and was in the middle of an intense fantasy when someone banged on his front door. He bit his lower lip and turned off the water, grabbing a towel. "Just a minute," he called, hastily drying himself, and yanked on shorts and a T-shirt.

"What took so long?" Chippy asked as soon as he pulled open the door. "You got company? Is Bri here?" He winked and leaned closer. "Just say so and we'll take off."

"I was just cleaning up." Obie stepped back so Chippy and David could come in. "What are you guys doing here?" He didn't think they had anything planned.

"You've been quiet for days, so we thought we'd stop over, find out what was up, and maybe see if you wanted to go out." David flopped on the sofa, and Chippy took one of the chairs and set a bag on the table. "We also brought the stuff for cosmos."

"You could have called or texted," Obie said as he went to his room to change. By the time he returned, drinks had been mixed and one sat on the coffee table waiting for him. "But I suppose this was better." He needed his friends.

"It is," Chippy agreed, raising his already half-empty glass. "Much better." He sat back, taking another sip of his drink. "So how are things with tall and hunky?"

Obie quickly decided to try to defuse the situation. "He's a client, you both know that."

David seemed content to let the subject drop, but Chippy could be like a dog with a bone if he thought there was a chance of getting any juicy gossip. "Come on, really? Some guy gives you shit on the court, and suddenly he was up and over there like a shot, crutches and all. Zoom." He motioned with his hands and nearly spilled his drink on Obie's sofa. "So, what's the real deal?" He leaned forward, and David did the same.

"We don't keep stuff from each other," David added, playing the guilt card beautifully. "So spill. Has he rocked your world yet?"

Obie rolled his eyes. "No. Nothing like that has happened."

"Why not? And don't give me this client excuse." Chippy turned to David. "God, it's like he's stuck in the fifties and Fonzie is going to come through that door any second." Chippy paused. "Though I think Fonzie was super hot with that leather jacket."

"Yeah, we know. You used to fantasize about him while we watched Nick at Nite reruns," David teased with a dramatic eye roll. "Try to focus on the topic at hand. Maybe make yourself useful and see if Obie has something to munch on before you get sloppy drunk."

Chippy huffed and set his glass on the table. "I'll get something in a minute," Obie said. It looked like they were settling in for the long haul, which was fine.

"So what's the dirt?" Chippy pressed.

"Bri is a client."

"Who likes you," Chippy added, cocking his eyebrow and looking like he'd sit there till doomsday waiting for Obie to talk. And it was easier to give in than to fight it.

"Nothing is happening. He's a client and he isn't really out." He didn't want to go through all this in great detail. "So we talked about it and decided that we'll see where things stand once he's healed and has a chance to decide what he truly wants." God, that sounded lame, even to him. "Just leave it alone, guys," he added with a sigh. "It doesn't matter what I want. Not really. He is a client, and I have a reputation to uphold. He's a professional athlete, and that's what's really important to him. So it doesn't matter that he's amazing, or that he took me to meet his parents…. His dad is a hoot and a half, by the way."

"You met his parents? When?" David asked, as though a little stunned.

"Sunday. He invited me to go along with him."

David shook his head. "And when did you make this little decision? Afterward, I bet." He shook his head as though Obie was the stupidest man on earth. "He took you to meet the folks because he likes you, and you threw cold water on it with all this crap. Babycakes, the heart wants what the heart wants. So, don't get physical until he's not a client, but call him, see if he wants to go to dinner or something, date, get to know each other, and if things get interesting…." David cocked his eyebrows.

"You're all about when things get interesting," Obie retorted.

"And you used to be too," Chippy interrupted. "You must really like this guy if you're willing to take this kind of chance." Chippy settled in his chair. "He's a famous athlete who isn't out of the closet, but he's coming to terms with who he is. Now, he can do that with you, or have every gay man in Philadelphia beating a path to his door. And believe me, they will be, as soon as word gets out. And it will get out. People saw you at the game, and they'll put two and two together fast enough."

Obie felt himself pale. "They will." *Shit.* "Look, you guys can't tell anyone. That's another reason why this has to stay professional. Bri needs to be able to figure out who he is on his own, just like the rest of us did."

David and Chippy looked at each other for two seconds before bursting into laughter. "We all came down the birth canal singing show tunes and you know it. There was no hiding for any of us. We're all gold-star gays. The only time we touched girl parts was when we were born."

David stuck his nose in the air. "I'm a platinum-star gay. Mom had me by cesarean."

"Please," Obie groaned. "We still had a choice to tell others. He should have that same choice. But if we're seen together a lot, then people will talk and his choice will be taken away."

David's grin slipped from his face. "Either you're crazy or you're falling in love with this guy. I'm not sure which. But with all this selflessness, I'm going with the latter. You like him, you really do. But maybe, just maybe, you should talk to him and ask what he wants."

"We did. And this is what we agreed to," Obie said, draining his glass, because damn it all, he needed a drink to calm his insides, which were turning loops now constantly.

"You did?" David asked. "Really." He turned to Chippy. "I bet he gave him that 'I'm a professional' speech and the 'what would people say if they found out I slept with my clients' thing."

Obie growled under his breath. "He did," Chippy said with a giggle. "That was the same speech he gave Kyle and Andy."

"Yeah, but that was just to put them off. He wasn't really interested in them. Maybe he's falling for his own propaganda now." David clicked his tongue, and Obie wanted to smack both of them.

"Just stop it. I'm right here," Obie snapped.

"Yeah, but we're right, aren't we? Sometimes you make things sound so reasonable, but it isn't what you really want. You're trying to delude yourself because you don't want to get hurt. Well, none of us does. That's natural. But what's going to hurt worse? You not giving this a chance, or taking one and having it not work out? Because that's the real choice. And before you pooh-pooh me, what if it does work out?"

"Yeah." Obie couldn't help smiling.

David clapped him on the leg. "Then think about that. Everyone knows you aren't going to sleep with your clients. So you take it slow, but don't write this off." They both looked at each other and nodded. "We saw the way he looked at you."

"Okay." Obie put his hands up in surrender. "I'll talk to him."

"Maybe ask him to dinner. The way to a man's heart is through his stomach," Chippy said and then giggled again. "Well, the fastest way to a man's heart is through his—"

"That's enough," Obie interrupted. The guys needed some food in their stomachs. They were already getting a little loopy.

"Come on. My Gran is almost ninety and she and Gramps have been married for over sixty years. At the big party last year, my mom asked her the secret to her long marriage. Do you know what her answer was? My mom nearly choked when she said it. 'A full stomach and empty balls.'" He broke into peals of laughter. "I thought my mom was going to die of embarrassment, but Gran had it right. Call him, invite him to dinner, and if it leads to something, so be it."

"You guys are worse than a couple of yentas," Obie protested, but not harshly. They cared and were his best friends. At least he had them in his corner.

"Speaking of yentas, have you talked to your mother?" Chippy asked.

"And when are you going to ask your parents to meet Bri? You already met his folks." Now the alcohol was definitely doing the talking.

"How about you let us take it one step at a time." Good lord, this was just what he needed. "All right? My dad would love to meet him, but you know Dad. He tends to put the cart before the horse sometimes." This was spinning way out of control, and Obie took a mental step back. He and Bri had kissed—nothing more. Yes, there was attraction—a stellar, black hole kind of gravity—but he was going to be governed by his big head, not the little one. That had gotten him in trouble before.

"How about you promise that you'll call him and ask him out," David said, crossing his arms over his chest.

"Yeah," Chippy said, piling on. "We can see the wishy-washy already creeping in. If you don't go for it, then you're a fool. We've been friends a long time and we know when you're scared and hiding." They shared a glance and then glared at him.

"I'll think about it, guys. God, it's not like either of you is an expert in relationships." Granted, he wasn't either, not by a long shot.

"No. We definitely suck in that department." David turned to Chippy. "I said suck." He giggled for a second. "But your luck is no better, and it's time that changed for one of us." He jumped off the sofa, returned with the pitcher of cosmos, and refilled glasses.

"God," Obie breathed.

"Let's see, there was Craig," David said, counting. "He was as interesting… as day-old bread." He ticked off on his fingers. "Victor…." He and Chippy shared another look.

"Victor was nice," Obie said defensively. Though the man could bore the wallpaper off the walls with all his talk of the mating habits of microscopic organisms. He was a professor of microbiology, and in the end, the last thing Obie wanted was for Victor's own mating habits to come anywhere near him.

"He was weirder than you thought," David said sheepishly.

Obie's mouth fell open. "You went out with him?" They never dated each other's exes. It was part of the twink code… if there was one. When your twink friend broke up with someone, you were indignant for your friend, but you never went out with the ex.

David swallowed hard. "I asked you, remember? You said it was okay and that he was nice." David leaned forward. "He was also really kinky and not in a good way. He had all these fetishes." He curled up his lip. "I can be as kinky as the next guy, but…."

Chippy snorted. "You are not. You're a vanilla sundae with vanilla sauce on top."

"Okay. Okay," Obie said, nearly losing his shit. This was what he needed, even if he hadn't realized it. An evening with the guys to laugh and let loose. He could figure out what he was going to do about Bri a little later. Right now, he needed to have fun.

"Let's watch a movie or something," Chippy suggested and grabbed the remote, turning on the television and flipping through channels. He stopped at *Meet Me in St. Louis* and sighed. "Isn't Judy just divine when she sings?" It was "The Trolley Song" and it was amazing. Obie settled back to watch, but David grabbed the remote and continued on.

"Go back," Chippy said, taking the remote from David as the commercial ended and the news came on.

"A fire was reported at the home of Philadelphia Rockets star Bri Early this afternoon...." Chippy flipped back to the movie, and Obie gasped, snatching the remote and turning the channel to the previous program. "The fire was confined to the garage. No estimate of damage has been released." Then they went on to another story.

Obie jumped to his feet, spilling his drink down the front of him. He swore and set the glass aside, picking his phone up off the table and hurrying from the room toward the stairs. He brought up Uber, arranged for a pickup, and was already pulling off his wet clothes by the time he reached his room.

"Where did you go? Did you call him?" David called up the stairs. Obie already had fresh pants and a shirt on, and the call to Bri was ringing as he hurried down the stairs, stopping to put on his shoes.

"There's no answer. I have an Uber coming. You guys stay if you want. I'm going over there." He made sure he had wallet and keys and was already heading to the door as the song in the movie came to an end. "I'll call as soon as I know something." The car arrived, and Obie single-mindedly pulled the door closed just as David and Chippy grinned at each other. He didn't have a chance to wonder what that meant as he jumped in the car and asked the driver to get to Bri's house as quickly as possible.

CHAPTER 7

BRI STOOD in the backyard, the acrid smell of smoke burning his nostrils. Even the house stank, so he had windows open and was going to have to call one of those restoration companies to take care of the mess. "There's someone outside saying he's a friend of yours," one of the firefighters said. They had been good enough to help him stay out of sight with the throngs of television news crews around.

Bri hobbled out toward the front of the house. He waved as Obie saw him and hurried over. "What happened? Where are your crutches?"

"In my car, which was in the garage. Apparently it was damaged in the fire, and I can't get in there to get them." Shit, he felt like a fool and was angry as hell. He should have locked the garage door just as tightly as he closed up the house.

"Do you want some help to go inside? Does it smell? If you want, I could call someone to see about getting fans and stuff." Obie was speaking a mile a minute, and it seemed like he was just getting started. "I heard the news on TV and I rushed right over to make sure you were okay." He paused to take a breath, and Bri thought he might get a chance to answer. No such luck. "Have you called your mom and dad? They are going to hear about this and be really worried." He was already guiding Bri toward one of his lawn chairs.

Bri sat down and figured he'd give Obie a few minutes to wind down. "I'm fine," he said finally. "I was about to call the folks when you appeared." He smiled and calmed down further when Obie turned to him, his eyes filled with worry and concern. "Just relax. I'm okay. The fire wasn't too bad and they were able to put it out right away. The fire department said they want to investigate and they're going to need some time. Unfortunately, I'd had the house open to air it out, so it filled with smoke and…."

"Okay. Then you can come and stay with me for a few days. I have an extra room, and no one is going to know where you are unless you want them to." He blinked those huge blue eyes, and Bri's willpower caved almost instantly.

"Are you sure about this? What about all the things you said earlier?" Bri asked as his heart beat a little faster.

"Yes, I'm sure. I'm not going to let you stay in a smoky house, or a hotel where everyone would be gawking at you." He stood, looking him over. "We'll need to get you a new set of crutches first. I got here by Uber because I was with the guys, but I can get another one to take us back just as soon as you can leave." He was already up and hurried inside the house, returning with a couple bottles of water. He handed one to Bri, who took it, half staring. "You need to drink and stay hydrated at times like these." Obie patted his hand. "Was anything else damaged?" He seemed to be calming down. "I was so worried," he added softly.

"I'm sorry."

Obie shook his head. "What do you have to be sorry for? You didn't do this." He blew air out of his mouth. "Am I right in assuming that they think this was deliberate?"

"Yeah. Whoever is behind the messages apparently has sent another one." His right hand shook, and he held it with his left to steady it, trying to be strong and cover up for how his world seemed to have turned on its side. "That goddamned crackpot. What did I ever do to him?" Bri had wracked his brain to try to figure out who could be behind this crap and came up empty.

"You were an athlete in school, right?" Obie asked with a sense of caution that wasn't present a few minutes earlier when he'd fired off questions like a machine gun. "High school and college. That's how you got to where you are, right?"

"Yeah," Bri answered, drawing out the sounds. Obie looked at him out of the corner of his eye, as he seemed to find one of the boring, trimmed shrubs on the edge of the yard interesting. "What are you asking?"

Obie sighed. "Okay. You were a jock, and I have to ask because… well… did you do any jock things?" He looked at him without meeting his eyes, and Bri couldn't help squirming. "You know, stupid shit that makes you cringe when you think of it?" He almost sounded like he wanted to make himself smaller too.

Bri closed his eyes. "Yeah. It was high school and we were big, stupid balls of testosterone with only half a brain to control it." He turned away. "I did a lot of things I regret." Bri swallowed hard. "I wish I could take some of those dumb things back. But I haven't seen any of those people in years. They left high school and went on, just like I did."

"Mr. Early," a firefighter said, and Bri was never so relieved for an interruption. He was already sweating under his collar and soon his shirt was going to be wet through. "We have the fire completely doused and did a quick investigation. The fire marshal's office will be here in an hour to officially investigate, but there's no question this fire was deliberately set. We have notified the police and they are on their way." He shifted his weight from foot to foot. "I'm sorry about all of this." He was probably in his midtwenties and had the young man look of a puppy dog, eager as hell to please. "We'll get secured what we can, but we suggest you contact your insurance company. They'll send people over to help clean up once the investigation is complete." He bit his lower lip.

"Thank you." He could feel the energy draining out of him by the second, flowing away like a fast-moving river. "I'll be here to meet the police when they arrive."

The firefighter, whose badge read Howard, didn't go anywhere. "Ummm, do you think I could get your autograph? It's for my son." Now, if this guy had a kid, he must still have been in diapers, but Bri agreed and signed a piece of paper for him. Then he sat back in the chair, sighing, and closed his eyes. Sometimes he really did think about chucking it all in and moving to Alaska. Not that he minded the fans and the celebrity, but sometimes it got in the way. "Thank you."

"Howard!" one of the other men called sharply. "Leave Mr. Early alone and get back to cleaning up." Howard snapped to and hurried away. Bri closed his eyes and tried to will away the jitters that refused to settle. Someone had set fire to his car and tried to burn his house down… with him in it. Suddenly, he was finding it hard to breathe. His eyes widened and it took a great effort to get air into his lungs.

"Just relax," Obie told him softly. "It's going to be okay. You're safe and you're going to stay that way." The determination in Obie's eyes eased some of the tension gripping his chest. His hands shook and he placed them on his lap, gripping his legs to try to control them.

Moments later, he saw his mother pull up in front of the house. She raced over to him. "Honey, I just heard the news. I tried calling, but you didn't answer, so I hurried over." She paused, looking down at both of them. It took Bri's now-sluggish senses a few seconds to realize that Obie's hand was on top of his and that he was very close. "I see."

Bri sighed. "Is this really a problem, Mom?" he asked, because he couldn't believe that she was picking this moment to have an issue with something he had told her some time ago.

"No. It's just something I need to get used to, I guess." She didn't come closer, and Obie pulled away and stood before bringing over a couple more chairs. His mom sat across from him. "Are you all right?" she asked.

"I'm fine. My phone was dead. I was going to call you as soon as I charged it." God, Bri was tired and wanted to take a nap. Maybe he already had, and this was just a bad dream. "I wasn't hurt, but the house is filled with smoke. So I'm going to stay with Obie for a few days until it can be cleaned up and the mess in the garage taken care of. That is, once the police are done." And who knew how long that was going to take.

"You should come home with your dad and me." She glanced at Obie and then back to him.

"Dad doesn't need the additional stress, and really, neither do you. I'll be fine. Obie doesn't live far away, and we can get back here easily enough." The list of things he needed to do began growing in his mind, and he didn't need to add arguing with his mother to that list.

To his surprise, she didn't push it. "Okay." She patted his hand. "I'm sure you know what you're doing." She sent another of those side glances at Obie. "But don't you need to be careful? People will know… I know you and your father have talked about this, but are you ready for your… proclivities… to be common knowledge?" The way she said it made Bri feel dirty.

"Proclivities?" Obie asked and then giggled a little. "What is this, the fifties? Bri is the man he is, and that's in a large part due to you and his dad. Let him make up his own mind about things."

She leaned back. "I only meant that people will think differently about him when they find out."

Bri's eyes widened. He'd just realized something—his mother was a snob. "Are you worried what your friends will say? Not that any of that matters. I'm not going to come bounding out of the closet and make an announcement on Jerry Springer. But I'm not going to hide either. I've been hiding who I am for a long time and I can't do it anymore." Besides, he wasn't very good at it, if the messages from his stalker were any indication. "I want to be able to live my life, period."

Mom leaned forward. "Are you sure this is what you want? You have a few more years to play. Once you retire, you can come out and be an elder statesman of the game. But if you do it now, they might cut you from the team." She patted his leg. "You need to think about the consequences."

"Excuse me?" Obie jumped to his feet, hands on his hips, staring at Bri's mother in absolute shock. "I know things aren't perfect, but the organization isn't going to fire Bri because he's gay. Bri is a talented, great player and the team needs him."

"It's okay, Obie," he soothed. "What she said is true and I know it. There are a lot of things that could happen. We talked about this before, but…." He sighed. "I don't know how much longer I can keep hiding and I don't want to. So I'm going to let the chips fall where they may." Now that he'd made the decision, he felt as though a weight had been lifted off his shoulders… and then he was sure he'd throw up.

"Don't make any decisions now," Obie cautioned, which was nearly shocking. Bri had expected him to be jumping up and down with joy. "You have enough to deal with at the moment."

"I agree. Take your time—think things through and make sure you know what you want." His mom stood, and Bri thought she was going to leave. "It looks like everything is under control here, and I have to check on your father. He has a doctor appointment in an hour." She leaned down, kissing Bri on the forehead the way she had when he was a child. "You scared me half to death, but if you're able to argue with me, I know you're all right. Call me tomorrow to let me know if you need any help." She left the yard, and Bri watched her go, wondering how she could give him emotional whiplash in a matter of minutes.

"Your mom cares," Obie said softly. "And she's worried about you. I could tell by those little lines around her eyes." Obie was obviously the forgiving sort, even after getting a dose of his mother's shortness. "It's probably her way of covering up her nerves, the same way you hold your arm so it doesn't shake." He raised his eyebrows.

"I thought I was good at covering that kind of shit up. I'm a professional basketball player—I'm supposed to be able to handle extreme stress." Sometimes it surprised him how understanding Obie was about so many things.

"On the court. This is life stress, and it's coming at you from a whole different direction. No matter what anyone says, no one is going to be able to shrug off someone setting their house on fire." Obie put his hand over his mouth. "Damn. I should know when to keep my big mouth shut."

"It's okay." He liked Obie's mouth, especially his lips and how they tasted.

"Have you seen inside yet?" Obie asked softly. Bri shook his head and once again imagined the charred mess inside the garage and the shriveled hunk of molten metal that was what was left of his car. Of course, his imagination might be running a little away with itself.

"No. I'm scared to."

"It might not be that bad," Obie told him. "The car is likely a write-off, and the inside of the garage is probably blackened but it should be fixable. And the car was insured, right? You'll get a new one and we'll have the mess cleaned up and…."

Once again, Bri thought he was going to puke. "This is my mess, and you need to stay away from it." He suddenly remembered his last message. He didn't want whoever was after him to hurt Obie. That sent a chill racing through him. "Maybe I should stay with my mom and dad." At least if he did that, Obie would be safe and whoever was behind this would leave him alone.

"If that's what you want," Obie said quietly and turned away. "I understand. I was only trying to help." Fuck, the aching hurt in his voice squeezed at Bri's heart. He hadn't wanted to hurt Obie, just keep him safe.

"What I want is for all of this to go away and my life to be the way it was. I want to play again and not have some psycho after me," he snapped. "I want to feel safe in my own house, which I probably never will again, and I want to know that you're safe and that…."

Obie slowly got to his feet, eyes as dark as storm clouds, lips pulled straight. "Was that stuff about going to your parents' some romantic notion about keeping me safe?" He wagged his hips. "I am not some damsel in distress that needs a knight in shining armor." Bri tried to keep a straight face but lost it.

"Damsel…." He reached for him, tugging Obie closer. "You are not any sort of damsel I have ever seen. Wrong parts." He smiled, looking up at Obie. "I don't want you hurt by all this."

"And I don't want you hurt by this. So we're even, and you can stop being gallant or whatever other bullshit is going through your head." He stepped back, and Bri's arms slipped downward and away. "So why don't you just say what you mean to say and let me make my own decisions." He rolled his eyes dramatically. "There. See, was that so hard?" His hands went back to his hips and he looked vaguely like Bri's third grade teacher who used to scold him for taking Susie's red crayon.

"Okay, okay. The last message hinted that something might happen to my friends. I didn't want you to get hurt so I thought it would be best if I distanced myself from you. That way whoever was doing this wouldn't have you in their sights. Okay, are you happy?" His snippy tone sounded immature, even to him.

"Yes. Thank you. And I appreciate that," Obie said. Bri sighed with relief. "Not that I'm buying it or going to let it happen. But I understand. And on the way back to my house, we'll stop to get you some new crutches. As soon as you can get in the house, we'll pack you a bag. If the clothes smell a little funky, we can put them right in the washer for you." Obie turned and began wandering back toward the garage. "I wonder how much longer they're going to be." He peered around the corner and then through the window at the back of the garage. "It looks like they're cleaning up and getting ready to go. At least the hunky firemen are…. The police just arrived."

"Great." Bri groaned as police officers stormed the backyard and then strolled up to him to ask a few questions. Yes, the car was insured. No, he didn't need money and wasn't having financial troubles. Yes, he had been receiving threatening calls. No, he didn't know who was behind them. Yes, he had been in the house when the fire had broken out, and no, he hadn't been aware until he smelled smoke and called the fire department right away. Yes, he had been out for a period of time that afternoon, and yes, he could account for his whereabouts. By the time they were done and Bri had answered enough questions to convince them that he hadn't set the fire himself, they seemed to get down to business. Meanwhile Obie's mouth hung open and he looked about ready to blow his top.

"Do you want me to call a lawyer?" Obie asked, arms folded over his chest. "Or maybe I should call Tweedledee and Tweedledum's supervisor, or even the mayor. Get some smart cops over here." Damn, Obie was a real firecracker when he was angry, and judging by the sparks coming from his eyes, these two were about to burst into flames at any second.

"And you are…?" Tweedledum asked.

"A friend of his. I have plenty of connections, so snap your brains into gear and do your jobs." He tapped his foot and glared at both of them. "I'm making a call anyway. This is ridiculous." Obie stormed off, and Bri wondered exactly who he intended to call. Obie returned a few minutes later and handed one of the officers the phone. Within minutes, the cop had gone completely pale as he stammered into the phone.

"Who did you call?" Bri asked, eyes widening by the second as the man on the phone turned a slight shade of green and looked about ready to lose the donuts he'd had for breakfast that morning.

"My father works in the police commissioner's office, so I made a call. Yes, they need to ascertain the facts of the case, but going so far as to accuse the victim of wrongdoing without a shred of evidence— hell, contrary to the evidence—is way out of line."

Bri was almost afraid to ask. "What does your father do? You said he works in the police commissioner's office. Is he his deputy or something?"

"Ummm." Obie bit his lower lip. "He's the police commissioner."

Bri swallowed hard and wondered if this was a joke. But then he looked at the two officers quaking in their shoes. The one handed the phone back to Obie and began consulting his notes.

"Why didn't you tell me?"

"You never asked, and I don't make a big deal about what my dad does. Lots of folks have powerful parents in this town, and I learned growing up that others try to trade on that." Obie leaned closer. "For years, the department in the city had a bad reputation. There were a lot of things that should never have happened. Dad's predecessor cracked down on internal corruption in a big way, and Dad has continued that work. Today the department is respected, and Dad really wants to keep it that way." Obie glared at the two men, who seemed to have had a complete attitude adjustment.

Their questions were respectful, and Bri got them to speak with the firefighter in charge. "I want to be able to get some things out of the house and go somewhere safe for a while. I'll give you copies of all the messages I've received, and you can check over the garage and house for any evidence you need. Just find out who did this." He was seconds from begging.

"Give them all your information, as well as ways to contact you," Obie prompted, and Bri provided that to the officers as well. "They can do their jobs." He glared at them, which was almost funny—slight, beautiful Obie making both men flinch with a pointed look. "We need to get you some new crutches and then off that leg for a while."

It took an hour before the police were done and Bri actually felt he could leave. Obie helped him to the waiting Uber, and they stopped to get him a fresh set of crutches. His clothes stank, and Obie promised he'd wash them. Once they got to Obie's place, he had Bri go on through, following behind him, but stopping to put in a load of laundry on the way.

"You don't need to clean up after me, I can—" Bri didn't get a chance to finish.

"It's fine." Obie hurried past where Bri had taken a seat on the sofa and ran up the stairs. "I put out towels in the bathroom for you. It has a soaker tub. I'm going to make some dinner. Why don't you go on up, fill the tub, and soak your leg for a little while? It will feel better."

"I'm fine."

Obie shook his head. "You had therapy today, and then all that excitement. Your muscles have got to be screaming about now. Go on and let them relax. When you come down, we can get something to eat and I'll give you a massage."

That sounded like heaven. Bri hobbled his way up the stairs and down the hall, following Obie's directions. The bathroom was stunning, with a deep tub that Bri filled. He stripped down and sank into the deep, hot water. He hadn't realized how much tension he'd been carrying in his leg, neck, and back until it relaxed. Bri lay back, closed his eyes, and tried not to think about the fact that someone was truly out to hurt him. Of course, as soon as he pushed that line of thought away, another came to the front. This one about five seven, slender, cute, with great lips and eyes, blazing red hair, and a set of hips that waved just a little when he walked.

Things heated up even more and Bri's hands slid down his chest, enclosing his length in a firm grip. A knock on the door made him jump, and he splashed some water out of the tub. "Yes." Did his voice just crack a little?

"I have a robe for you. I'm going to slip it inside the door." It opened slightly, and Obie hung the robe on the knob before closing the door again. "Come down as soon as you're ready."

Nothing else was going to happen, and after a few minutes, Bri got out of the tub, dried off, and put on the robe. His clothes smelled like smoke and he didn't feel like putting them on again, so he left the bathroom, crutching his way down the stairs. Obie was in the kitchen, getting dinner on the table. "I have the first load of laundry in the dryer." He turned and his mouth fell open, his lips moved, but no words came out.

"What?"

Obie swallowed and pulled out a chair. Bri sat down, pulling the robe closer around him. "You…."

"I see. Maybe I should just put the clothes I was wearing back on."

Obie nodded. "Yeah… you're…. On second thought, just stay the way you are. The view is amazing and I could watch it all day." Obie actually shivered and then shook his head, turning away, cheeks and neck going almost as red as his hair. "I can't believe I just said that."

Bri got to his feet, taking a few careful steps to where Obie stood near the stove. He gently slipped his arms around his waist. Obie grew still and stiffened; Bri felt him hold his breath. "I'm not going to hurt you."

"Of course not." Obie slowly turned around and held still. "I'm afraid this is a dream and that I'll wake up."

"It may be a dream, but I don't think either of us is asleep." A timer went off, and Bri just about screamed. Obie jumped and backed away.

"I need to get dinner out of the oven." He took a few shaky steps, and Bri sat back down before he lost his balance and hurt himself again. He also needed to adjust the robe so his dick didn't raise the terry cloth like a damned tent pole. He edged his chair under the table as Obie brought over a plate of baked pasta that made his stomach growl.

Obie fixed his own plate and sat across from him. "Do you want some wine?" Obie jumped up, racing to open a bottle. The glasses clinked as he got two out of the cabinet and he nearly tipped them as he set the glasses on the table. "God…," he muttered under his breath. "I'm sorry. But I'm nervous and…."

"There's nothing to be nervous about. Nothing is going to happen that you don't want to. I won't force you." He tried to keep from being affronted, and knew he was failing.

"I know that. And it isn't like I haven't had sex before, because I have. But it never meant something, like this might… or could… or…. Shit, just stick something in my mouth to shut me up." Obie must have realized what he'd said because he blushed something fierce once again and managed to sit in the chair without falling backward. He also stopped rambling and lowered his head to eat.

Damn, he was cute, especially when he got flustered. The most interesting things came out of his mouth, and Bri never knew what he was going to say. "You have nothing to be worried about." He reached across the table, Obie's fingers sliding into his. "Just relax."

"I tend to get verbal diarrhea when I get flustered. My dad always said that I could never follow in his footsteps because at the first sign of stress, I'd start blathering like an idiot and the criminals would hear me coming a mile away." He giggled nervously.

"I like it when you talk that way. Not that I want you to be nervous, but it's genuine… and honest." He tried to think of the words he wanted to say, taking a bite to cover his thoughtfulness. "I have dozens of people around me, all the time, that I can ask an opinion of… but the only opinion I'm going to get is mine. They tell me what they think I want to hear. And fans, they just want to get close and they tell me how great I am… all of that."

"But isn't that nice?" Obie asked.

"Of course it is. But it isn't honesty. The first therapist I had was so… awed that I was working with him that every time I flinched, he stopped. In the end, he did nothing to help me. Because I might get angry or… whatever. Sure, I might yell because it hurt, but I'm not afraid of hard work, and I may growl, but it doesn't mean I'm angry." It was hard for him to fully articulate what he was truly feeling. "I'm a person, just like everyone else."

"I think I understand. Everyone puts you on a pedestal because you're the great Bri Early." Obie swallowed and looked up from his dinner. "Was it that way in high school?"

"Oh, God yes. I was a really good player for my age. I led my team to victory one year after another. I could play circles around most other players and I scored big. Everyone wanted that to continue—it meant money for the school and lots of people coming to the games. It was the same in college. I was held up as someone important, and if I did something wrong, it was fixed. The coaches, the other players, teachers… everyone had a vested interest in me because I brought in money, and plenty of it." He set down his fork. "The thing was, I didn't even realize it was happening. Not all of it, anyway. I was a kid and I thought this was what was due to me. So I took it and let others clean up the messes."

"Did you make a lot of them?" Obie questioned as his gaze intensified. "I somehow can't see you as a problem player."

"I grew up. I had to, and I did it fast. See, there was an incident when I was a sophomore. It wasn't pretty. A group of players decided to go to New York on an off weekend in the schedule. They hired some ladies to serve as entertainment and they spent the weekend having the time of their lives. There was lot of drinking… as well as harder… shall we say, stress relievers—as many as half a dozen women. They broke up the hotel rooms and caused a lot of damage. I was there for some of it, but not all. I had an uncle in New York, and he took me to dinner the night it happened." Bri had never been so grateful for anything in his life. He had been away and he'd been able to prove it.

"What happened?" Obie asked. "It was more than broken up hotel rooms, wasn't it?"

Bri shook his head. "It was a lot more." He was barely able to whisper. "One of the girls, well, she had a specialty. She went off with one of the players so they could… play, and things got too rough. We were all pretty strong, and she got hurt really badly. The guys carried her out of the room and down the back stairs, and left her out back near the dumpsters, like she was a piece of trash." Bri felt like throwing up just thinking about it. He pushed his plate away and saw Obie doing the same. "I'm sorry. This isn't exactly dinner conversation." His head ached and he wondered why he had ever gone down this conversational road at all.

"Was she okay?" Obie asked and Bri nodded. "I take it she was found."

"Yeah. Some men from the hotel found her, called the police, and all hell broke loose about ten minutes after I got back. The police got us all up and brought us into one of the conference rooms, talking to everyone. I had just gotten back and was able to tell them where I'd been. They called my uncle to verify, and then they let me return to my room. The others… they didn't get off so lightly. Charges flew all over the place. Some of the guys weren't able to return, and even ended up in jail. The team got decimated, and the college was fined. They almost lost their basketball program. It was pretty bad. The team was tainted—and that meant me too, for a while. My uncle actually testified and even went with me to some of my pro interviews and 'meet and greets' to explain that I was with him when it all went down, just so they would know I had nothing to do with it." He never wanted to go through anything like that again. "That's when I grew up."

Obie nodded and swallowed hard. He took a tentative bite of pasta, made a face, and set his fork down again. Bri was no longer hungry. "Do you know what happened to her?"

"Not really. I know she recovered. I heard on the news that she'd been a runaway, and there were reports that her family found her and took her home. She went by the name Charity, but I bet that wasn't her real name. Still, it was the only one we knew. I hope she was able to go on with her life… somehow." He pursed his lips slightly. "Everyone has that moment when they learn that life isn't what they expected and that what they thought was true is really a huge crock of crap. That was mine." Bri picked up his fork, even though his appetite was gone. "I really haven't thought about all this in quite a while."

"Do you think this stalker you've got might be somehow connected to that incident?" Obie asked. "I mean, I suppose it's a long shot, and you weren't even there."

"I've thought about that. I don't remember her name, but the last I heard, Charity had gone back home to live with her parents. She testified in court and then she left. I don't think she'd come back to try to get even with me. Some of the guys went to prison, while I finished college and then went on to the pros." He'd often wondered what had happened to her.

"Maybe she had relatives," Obie offered.

"I don't know. That was a long time ago. If something was going to happen, why now? Why not all those years ago? And I never even saw the girls. I was just the teammate of a bunch of guys who couldn't behave." He ate slowly, continuing to think.

"You're probably right, and I'm sorry I made you go over that again." Obie reached across the table, taking his hand gently. "I'm sorry you got caught up in that mess." Obie finished eating and carried his plate to the sink. He hurried from the room and returned with a laptop, sitting back down and opening the lid. He typed for a while, then turned to Bri.

"Her real name was Charity Collins. The later news stories ran it. Apparently, she returned to Lancaster with her family." Obie continued typing. "She's married now and has two children." Obie turned the screen to display a picture on Facebook. It was a photo of a woman, surrounded by her husband and two young kids. "It looks like she's happy, and that she's gone on with her life, judging from her posts and pictures." Obie clicked a few times. "She really needs to adjust her privacy settings, but there's nothing here to suggest that she'd want to come to Philly to set your house on fire."

Bri watched as Obie looked through the posts. "At least it seems as though she has a good life."

"And people with good lives don't usually hurt others—at least not intentionally." Obie closed the computer. "I was hopeful that we might find out something. I guess it's always possible, but it doesn't seem likely that she'd be your stalker." He seemed flustered and drummed his fingers on the lid of the laptop. "There has to be a reason behind this. If we find it, we might get closer to figuring out who this nutjob is." His fingers continued their rhythmic patter.

"I wish I knew. It isn't like I go around pissing people off all the damn time. Though I sure got someone mad at me." He ate the last of his dinner, and Obie took care of the dishes as the dryer dinged. Obie hurried away and returned with some of Bri's clothes, folded and in a pile, mercifully free of the smell of smoke. He set down the clothes in the next chair and turned away, stiffly going back to loading the dishwasher, the plates clanging as he did. "This is a difficult subject for you, isn't it?" Bri asked.

"Well, yeah. I mean, my being gay was no secret. It took everyone about two seconds to figure it out, and with this hair…." Obie didn't look at him. "High school was pretty much hell, especially since I kept as much shit as I could from my dad." His shoulders stiffened, and Bri levered himself onto his feet, using the crutches to steady him.

"I'm sorry. I know I didn't do my share in trying to make school an easy experience for a lot of people." He groaned and wiped his hand down his face. "Lord knows if I had just said who I was, there would have been a lot of shit thrown…."

"Yeah, probably. But you were a jock and really good. You'd have weathered it and come out smelling like a rose on the other side…." Obie slowly turned around. "But maybe you wouldn't have gotten into the college you did. Or maybe the professional scouts would have discounted you the way they have other people. I really do get that. But there was no way they were going to squeeze you into a locker and try to close it on you." Obie sighed. "Whatever happened to me, none of it was your fault. And when my dad did find out…."

"Fireworks?" Bri asked.

Obie nodded. "You have no idea. He was down on the people at the school like a big papa bear. They instituted an antibullying program and even helped me start a gay/straight alliance at the school. Some parents objected—you know the type—but I had support, and that's all that mattered." He sighed loudly. "None of that has anything to do with you, and I'm only bringing it up because even today, if I met my bully, Kevin Webster, in public, it would take a great deal of restraint to keep me from kicking him in the nuts." He held Bri's gaze almost until it became uncomfortable.

"I didn't pick on people like that. Classes were already really hard for me, and you can imagine Mom and Dad weren't particularly thrilled with that. Dad kept hoping I would apply myself and my grades would improve. So every report card was a hardship because I didn't want to disappoint him. Who wants to be the dumb one in the family?" Bri turned away and stared at the oak graining in the tabletop. "I studied hard because Mom and Dad weren't going to allow me to slough off. We had a deal. If I wanted to play, I had to keep my grades up." He closed his eyes, remembering some of the kids who were picked on. Kids like Obie might have been. "There was a guy, Pat, who liked to pick on kids, one in particular. God, he was one mean son of a bitch. Pat was huge, and he thought anyone smaller than him was fair game. Pat was also about as smart as a box of rocks."

"Do you remember the kid he picked on?" Obie asked softly.

"Not really. He was sort of tall, a beanpole kind of kid, with blond hair, and he talked with a slight lisp. I remember seeing him a few times, usually sitting by himself. He was smart, and he had a few friends. Funny, I remember thinking how bad I felt for him. I was pretty sure he was gay too, but I was too cowardly to go up and try to befriend him." Bri pulled the robe around him tightly, as though it were a sort of armor against the past. "Sometimes being young and stupid really sucks."

Obie nodded. "Amen to that."

"I wish I had met someone like you back then," Bri admitted.

"Why? I doubt we would have been friends." Obie was right, of course. Bri would have stayed away from him like the plague. "Fear sucks, and it robs us of a lot of things."

"What do you mean?" Not that he could argue with him.

"What if the kid that Pat picked on was meant to be the best friend you ever had?" Obie asked. "What if he was gay and turned out to be your other half? The one you were destined for? That special person who understood you more than anyone else? But because you were afraid to approach him, you never found out?" Obie took a step closer. "It strips away possibilities because we don't have the courage to kick it in the ass and tell it to bugger off. Not that I was the most courageous person. There was a guy I liked in high school and I never approached him either. I didn't want to get rejected or my face bashed in."

Bri couldn't help chuckling. "I think we were all in the same boat, if in a different way." He shifted the crutches under his arm, trying to hold on to his freshly laundered clothes. He nearly dropped them, and Obie caught the small pile before it spilled over the floor.

"I have them." He straightened the clothes and followed as Bri hobbled into the living room. "I didn't mean to have such a serious conversation. If I made you uncomfortable, I'm sorry."

Bri sat down, and Obie handed him the clothes. "Maybe I needed that conversation. Someone hates me, and though I don't know why, there has to be a reason." He picked up his phone when it vibrated, but when he didn't recognize the number, he declined the call. He half suspected it might be his stalker, but the thought of hearing that voice again made his stomach churn.

"If there is, we'll find it," Obie told him. "I'm going to give you a few minutes to put on your shorts and then you can meet me in the therapy room." The phone beeped to indicate that he had a voicemail. Bri didn't even want to look and handed the unlocked phone to Obie.

"It's from your dad," Obie said. Bri wondered about the strange number, then listened to the brief message and called his dad back.

"What's up? Did you get a new phone?"

"Yes. I told your mother that we could have the same number, but she must have forgotten. The old one went on a diving expedition." Meaning, his dad had dropped it in the toilet... again. "I wanted to see how you were. Your mother said you were okay, but I was still worried."

"I'm with Obie, and he's looking after me. The police are going over my house pretty thoroughly now." He smiled and relayed the story of the two cops.

"I knew he had hidden depths," his dad said about Obie. "Let him help you, and you call if there are any more messages. Did you give what you had to the police?"

"Yes, and Obie mentioned it to his dad, so they're taking it seriously." He swallowed hard. "Obie thinks that the injury in the game was deliberate, and I'm starting to think so too. I don't know why...." Obie tapped him on the shoulder, motioning to where he was going with his own phone, then left the room. "Obie seems to think it could be someone from school."

"Not that girl who was hurt?" his dad asked.

"It could be her. She always blamed me, even though I wasn't there. She'd said she heard the guys talking about it, saying I would have loved it. So in her mind, I came up with the idea. You know. But I keep going through my past. The guy on the team that keeps coming to mind is Donald, but I doubt he has the smarts to pull this off."

"You be careful and watch your back. Call if you need anything." His dad ended the call, and Obie hurried into the room.

"What is it?" Bri asked.

"My dad is on his way over," Obie announced. "So you might want to get dressed. He said he wants to talk to you and...." Obie bit his lower lip. "I asked him to come over so he could look into this personally. He also said he has some more information for you." Obie was suddenly filled with energy, hurrying around to pick up and put things away, not that the house was messy by any means. Then he started fussing in the kitchen while Bri got dressed and hung the robe in the bathroom.

111

Just as he got settled on the sofa, he heard a knock on the front door. Moments later, a large man strode inside. "Hey, Dad." Obie met him and they exchanged a brief hug. "This is Bri Early. Bri, James Kenoble." Obie hurried out and brought in a tray with drinks and some crackers and cheese, setting it on the table.

Bri extended his hand, grateful that Obie's dad didn't stand on ceremony and sat right away. "What can I do for you, commissioner?" he asked.

"It's what I can do for you." He reached for a cracker and took a small bite. Bri watched him and saw the similarity between Obie and his dad. He had graying red hair, though it wasn't the bright color of Obie's that he liked so much. But they did share the same intense eyes and warm smile. "I want to apologize for the officers this afternoon. It should've been fairly obvious what had happened, and they were overzealous. We're making sure they get the training they need." He nibbled on the cracker as Obie hovered nearby a little nervously.

"Okay. But I'm assuming you didn't come over here just to apologize. Besides, it was Obie who stood up to them. You should have seen him." Bri laughed outright. "Those two nearly pissed themselves when he handed them the phone." He took a deep breath and calmed himself. "So what did you find?"

"Your car was laced with plenty of accelerant. If it hadn't been compromised, the garage and probably the house would have gone up like a torch. As it was, the powder just fizzled. We believe that the perpetrator emptied the powder out of a number of bullets, but it had been stored somewhere damp so little happened." He sat back and finished his cracker.

"Do you want something to drink, Dad?" Obie asked even as he handed a glass to Bri, lightly touching his shoulder.

"No, thanks. I'm fine." He turned back to Bri. "We believe this is an amateur who probably saw something on television and got a bright idea."

"Have you got a line on who might have done this?" Bri asked.

"We're getting there and working additional evidence." He was hedging; Bri could feel it. "We're also working over what we can on the phone calls and messages. We've narrowed them to a burner phone and we're tracing where it was sold to see if we can get a customer. I wish I had more news for you, but sometimes, these things take time." He lifted his gaze to Obie. "Both of you need to be careful. I can assign an officer to stay here with you." He pulled out his phone.

"Dad, no. If I have police here, it's going to make it hard for me to work with my clients." He turned to Bri. "What do you think? It would be more protection." He bit his lower lip the way he did when he was nervous.

"Do you really have the manpower for that?" Bri asked. "Obie and I should be fine. Anyone would be stupid to try anything here. If you increase patrols in this area, that should be enough. We'll promise to call right away if anything happens or if I get another message." God, the last thing he wanted was for his life to be more disrupted than it already was. "How long before you think I can go home?"

"We'd like a few more days to go over everything. Whoever did this didn't know how to set a fire, but they were very good at covering their tracks." He leaned closer. "At every crime scene, each person leaves traces of themselves, even if they don't mean to. We have found a few clues, including where they broke in and got into your car. We'd like a little more time, if that's all right?" Not that he needed to ask, but it was good that he did. To Bri, it showed the kind of person he was.

"Of course. I want to catch this guy." Up until now, Bri had been doing a pretty good job of covering the tornado of fear and worry that kept welling and receding in his gut. But now his right hand shook, and he held it with the other, though it made no difference. "I want to be able to fix up my home and live there again. This is…."

Obie put his arms around him from behind, his hands sliding over Bri's shoulders and then resting on his chest. "It's okay. You're safe," he whispered.

"Am I?" Bri asked. "Really?" He turned to James. "I don't know if I'll ever be able to be safe again—not in my own home, not on the basketball court. Hell, every time my phone rings, I worry that it's this asshole calling to taunt me." A dam seemed to burst inside him, pulling away the last of his control. Bri wanted to cry but he'd be damned if he was going to do that in front of the fucking police commissioner. He took a deep breath and did his best to regain some modicum of control.

"We're going to do our best. We have a police presence at your house and we will all night and into tomorrow. Have you called your insurance company?" James asked, and Bri nodded.

"They're waiting for you to finish the investigation," he explained. "We have an appointment to meet tomorrow. I hoped that would be enough time, but...."

"It will be fine," James agreed and then turned to Obie. "Are you going to be all right?"

"Yes, Dad. I'm fine."

The police commissioner's eyes hardened. "And how long have you and Mr. Early been seeing each other?" The tone was harsher than Bri expected, and he was pleased he wasn't on the receiving end of the question.

"Dad," Obie replied gently. "Bri is a...." He faltered and his breath turned to a sigh. "Look. Bri is a client. I'm helping him recover from an injury. I like him and I think he likes me. But nothing has happened between us. We're just getting to know one another." He swallowed and leaned forward so Bri could see him. "Bri's feelings are private, as are mine, and...."

That hawkish look shifted to him, and Bri's leg quivered. "You're not out and open about who you are?" It was almost a demand.

"It's not that easy. He's—" Obie argued, but Bri nodded. This was his issue, not Obie's. Bri shouldn't let Obie take the heat for it.

"I'm not out, no. I have a few years to play and...." Damn, now he couldn't seem to put together a sentence that didn't sound lame.

"So you intend to hide and want Obie to hide along with you? Is that the idea?" Obie's dad leaned closer, a slightly smug expression on his face, as though he had everything figured out.

"Enough, Dad. Why do you think I didn't tell you about this?" Obie straightened up. Clearly this had been what he was worried about and why he'd been nervously bustling around the house before his dad arrived. "I know you want to protect me, but you can't always do that. Bri has the right to figure out who he is and come out at his own speed, when *he* feels the time is right." Damn, his eyes held the same fire as his father's. It was exciting, especially the way he fought for him. "He has friends who know and support him. It's just the greater world who isn't aware, and that's fine for now."

"What about his parents?" James asked, with a little less vehemence.

"My dad is really supportive. Mom has a harder time with it, but they do their best to understand. They're proud of me." Bri wasn't sure what to say. Obie gripped his hand tightly, giving Bri the silent support he needed. "I never wanted to face who I was. I dated women for most of my life. I tried like hell to deny who I was attracted to for a long time. I kept my head down, studied, practiced until my feet bled. Being a basketball player was all I ever wanted, and I made it. I couldn't throw it away." His mouth went dry. "Can you imagine how much court time I'd have gotten if I had come out of the closet in college? Exactly zero. I know that. I wasn't as worried about how everyone else would feel, but the other players, the coaches... the league... I'd be frozen out." He squeezed Obie's fingers and released them. "So I kept my mouth shut and played the best I could each and every game."

"And now...." James leaned closer, those eyes piercing and bright. "What are your plans? It's plain my son has feelings for you, and I fear they may be interfering with his ability to see clearly." He pushed his glasses up on his nose. "This is the young man I fought for, the son I did anything to protect, just so he could be himself. That's all that has ever mattered to me, that my son could be the man he is and not have to hide part of himself."

"I have...." Bri was about to argue but couldn't. He was hiding, and that required anyone he was with to hide as well. "I'm a gay man trying to figure things out." He stopped, realizing that this was the first time he had ever used those words. "And everything isn't cut and dried."

"Dad, I think this is enough," Obie snapped. "You just met him, and he's been under a lot of stress. Is now really the best time for us to have this conversation?" Obie glared, and to Bri's surprise, his father nodded and sat back.

"A chip off the old block, that one," James said, pride ringing in his voice.

Bri turned to catch Obie's gaze. "Sometimes it amazes me how strong you are. Like a tiger or something."

"My boy never took much crap from anyone," James said. "Not even me." James handed him a card. "If you have any questions about the case, feel free to call me. I'll do my best to keep you up to date." He stood. "As for the rest, I'll do my best to keep my nose out of my son's business, but I can't guarantee anything."

Bri nodded. "Actually, I do have just one question." He couldn't help it. "What possessed you to name him Obie Juan Kenoble?"

"Bri," Obie whispered and James grew serious before smiling and then chuckling.

"They're family names, and I figured if I gave him a name like that, no one would forget him. Sometimes in this world, all it takes to be successful is to be remembered. Besides, I loved those movies, and that character was wise and willing to make the tough choices. That's someone to respect and admire." James clapped Obie on the shoulder. "He's more than lived up to it." He turned and headed for the door, leaving them both speechless.

"DAMMIT TO hell!" *I can't take it any longer. My head hurts so bad, I can't see straight. They told me the house and garage were supposed to go up like a Roman candle with everything I packed in there. He was home when it went off. I even screwed up the gunpowder. Next time, there won't be any mistakes.*

"… All reports are that Mr. Early, while home during the incident, wasn't injured in the fire."

"*Shit!*" A crack fills the room, and I drop the remote to the floor in pieces.

CHAPTER 8

OBIE STARED after his father. He had always hated his name and did his best to keep it a secret. He'd certainly never thought of it in the way his father had just said. "I guess I should take care of all this." He needed a second alone to digest what had just happened. "I'll be right back." He grabbed the handles of the enameled tray and hurried to the kitchen.

"You know, your dad is pretty cool," Bri called after him.

"You're not upset or embarrassed all to hell?" He knew he was. "Dad doesn't have much of a filter when it comes to certain things, especially me. You could give him access to all the nation's secrets and he'd never utter a word. But if it has anything to do with me, my dad doesn't seem to be able to shut up."

"He cares about you," Bri said as he crutched his way into the kitchen. "Now I know where you get your spirit from." He smiled as Obie looked over his shoulder to see if Bri was teasing him. He didn't seem to be. "Don't be embarrassed by your dad. I liked him. He sure knows how to give a guy a kick in the ass, though." Bri rubbed his backside for effect.

"Don't let him get under your skin. Dad takes things pretty seriously." It was part of the reason Obie didn't introduce his dad to his friends right away. He had a tendency to scare them off.

"You have a lot in common with your dad," Bri said, and Obie whirled around.

"I do not!" he said almost vehemently and turned away once again before Bri could give him the stink eye. "Dad is… he was always supportive… militantly so. When he found out I was being bullied, he got involved. But still, it was hard as hell being the kid of the police commissioner."

Bri stood his ground, listening. Obie had to give him credit—he didn't load him up with a bunch of platitudes.

"He was in a position of power. That meant that the big guys in school thought picking on me gave them greater status. They were brave enough to bully the police commissioner's kid. I didn't want Dad to know because I didn't want him to think I was weak and useless. So I kept it from him until it got bad. When it did, Dad came down on everyone. Yeah, he helped me set up the alliance and all, but things were still bad a lot of the time." Obie wiped his hands on a dish towel. "None of that was his fault. I know that now, but I still blamed him for it." God, sometimes teenage thinking could mess you up bigtime. "He and I worked things out some time ago, but it's still hard to get stuff straight in my head."

Obie took a step. Bri opened his arms, letting his crutches fall to the floor with a metal *tink*, and Obie came closer. Bri's strong arms wrapped around him, holding tightly. He didn't say anything, just held him, and Obie buried his nose in Bri's shirt, inhaling deeply. When he lifted his gaze to make sure this was all right, Bri's met his, heat sparked, and he went up on his tiptoes to get closer.

Bri closed the distance between them, kissing him hard, energy surging, setting every cell in Obie's body on fire. He held on to him, and he'd probably have climbed Bri like a tree except for his bad knee.

"Your crutches," he mumbled and reluctantly backed away.

"You're really going to worry about those right now?" he asked.

"I don't want you to get hurt," Obie said, scurrying to pick them up and get them back under Bri's arms. "I want you as healthy and out of pain as possible." Then he was there once again, holding Bri, their kisses intensifying quickly. "Why don't we turn out the lights and go upstairs?" His heart pounded loudly enough that he could hear it, and he hoped to hell he wasn't making a fool of himself. Bri nodded, and Obie waited for him to leave the room, switching out the lights before going up the stairs, watching Bri's ass as he took each step.

At the top of the stairs, Bri paused, turning toward him. "Which room?"

Obie paused. He'd assumed that Bri was interested in sleeping with him. They had been hot and heavy, but maybe…. "Which one do you want?" he asked sheepishly.

Bri balanced on the crutches, leaning closer. "Let me be clear—which room is yours?" His eyes blazed with heat and his voice sent shivers up and down Obie's spine. He blinked and motioned to the door at the end of the hall. Bri maneuvered his way to the door and opened it. "Wow," he said.

"I know. Don't you love it?" The bedroom was his favorite room in the house. The furniture was all dark wood, with light gray walls, and a huge, deep red comforter that looked as divine and decadent as anything he had ever seen. Obie had found it on a trip to Dallas a few years ago and had paid quite a bit for it, but still thought it was worth every penny.

"Man…." Bri entered the room and set his crutches against the wall, then sat on the edge of the bed, slowly lying back. "Oh my God. It's like I'm on a cloud."

"Exactly. And it's a new age material, so it isn't anywhere near as warm as you'd think it would be." He slipped off his shoes and climbed onto the bed, lying on his back, looking up at the ceiling. Shoes thunked to the floor, and Bri sighed. "I'm a little worn out." He lay back and didn't move, breathing deeply. Obie slipped off the bed and carefully removed his brace, setting it near the crutches.

"How is that?" Obie asked.

"Heavenly. Whenever I take that off, it feels like I'm getting my leg back, at least for a while." Obie lay down once again, and Bri's hand slipped into his. Neither said anything, even as Obie's heart beat faster, but he didn't want to make waves or change the mood. Obie had brought a few guys to his room, but that was mostly for sex. They hadn't just stayed there, lying side by side quietly, simply being happy. There was something to be said about having someone he could do nothing with in bed.

After a few minutes, Bri got up and hobbled out the door and to the bathroom, insisting he could do it himself. Obie sat up, wondering what he should do. Should he get undressed and be waiting for Bri to come back? But what if he needed help getting to the bed? Bri didn't have his brace and crutches. More unsure of himself than he'd ever been, Obie took off his socks and put away the laundry. Then he heard the water go off.

He stood, waiting for the door to open, but wasn't at all prepared to see Bri standing in the bathroom doorway wearing only a towel. Damn, just damn. His throat went dry as thick, corded muscles rippled with each movement Bri made. He was gorgeous, and Obie could barely believe his eyes. He had wondered many times what Bri looked like under his team jersey and shorts, even his jeans and shirt, but every single one of his imaginings had come up short. "Do you need help getting back to the bedroom?" he asked, forcing his voice to work.

At his nod, Obie hurried over and took Bri's arm, his heat and damp skin sliding under his hand. "Thanks."

"Yeah." He tried not to look as the towel shifted with each of Bri's steps. Finally, though it was only a few minutes at most, they were in the bedroom, and Obie had Bri seated once more on the side of the bed.

"I'm going to use the bathroom too. I'll be right back." He hurried away, because he was seconds from jumping the man, and scampered into the bathroom, closing the door. He stripped off his clothes, freeing his throbbing cock, and quickly brushed his teeth. Then he stepped into the shower, rinsing off quickly, drying his skin, and checking in the mirror that he didn't look too freakish. His hair was even redder now that it was wet, and he looked downward. His chest wasn't defined and full like Bri's, and he was skinny and pale, where Bri was tall, muscular, and hot as all hell. Still, hiding in the bathroom wasn't going to do him any good. He turned off the lights and grabbed a towel, wrapping it around his waist before opening the door.

He stepped into the bedroom and paused. Bri had turned out all the lights but a small one next to the bed. The glow shone off his skin where he lay on the white sheets, half drawn up to just cover his butt, back and arms stretched out. The sheet clung to him, accentuating the curves of what was hidden underneath the covers. Obie gasped and covered his mouth to keep a squeak from sneaking out. "Are you still going to give me that massage?" Bri asked, seemingly half asleep, but Obie had an idea that Bri was just as awake as he was, especially judging by the way his leg shook just a little under the sheet.

Damn, that excitement was hot. Obie approached and pulled open the drawer of the nightstand, getting out a small vial of cinnamon oil before closing the drawer again. Then he climbed onto the bed and sat next to Bri. He rubbed a little oil into his hands and then placed them on Bri's shoulder blades. He jumped slightly and settled again, breathing deeply as Obie rubbed in the oil, encouraging the muscles to relax and let go of their tension.

"You have magic hands, you know that?" Bri stretched out farther as Obie stroked the corded muscles of his back and down to his hips.

"I try," Obie whispered and continued working his back. "You really need to learn not to carry your tension in your shoulders. The muscles are in knots." He worked deeply inside Bri's shoulders and then moved down his back to the curve of his butt. He hesitated before slowly sliding the sheet downward. Holy cow. His hands smoothed over firm cheeks and he groaned deep in his throat. Obie flipped the sheet off Bri's legs, exposing his entire backside to his ravenous eyes. His hands slipped and he giggled nervously.

"What are you doing?" Bri grinned as he half rolled over, his eyes dark and deep with passion.

"Your hotness sort of overtook me." He leaned down and kissed Bri. "You know, I'm used to doing these on my table down in the office, not up here in my bedroom." He patted Bri's butt and went back to work, smooth skin flowing under his hands as he kneaded and massaged the perfect globes.

Bri sighed softly when he shifted to his legs. For the time being, Obie put all of Bri's hotness out of his mind as he worked his injured leg. "You know, if you keep that up you'll turn me to Jell-O." He groaned as Obie finished the first leg, starting to work on the second.

Then Bri did something amazing, stupendous, breath-stealing—he rolled over.

Obie nearly swallowed his tongue for a second and then found his voice. "What exactly do you want me to massage?" His attention drifted from Bri's eyes, down his strong chest, to the long, thick cock that was stretching most of the way to his belly button. Damn. Just... damn. He winked, and Bri sat up, tugging the towel away from his waist and pulling Obie down on top of him.

"How about—" He slid his hands down Obie's back, cupping his butt. "—you and I put the massage on hold." He guided Obie's lips to his, kissing him deeply. "I think I've wondered what this would be like ever since I saw you dancing at the club."

"Me?" Obie breathed.

"Oh yeah. You moved this tight body, got me wondering things I was afraid of." He held Obie tighter, flexing his hips slightly under him, their cocks sliding together. "You made me watch you just by the way you moved."

Obie swallowed hard. "And now?" He stiffened. "I'm not dark and tan like you. I'm sort of pasty and pale and—"

"You're stunning," Bri told him, running his fingers through Obie's hair. "I watch you all the damn time." He drew Obie closer, heat building as Obie closed his lips over Bri's. He felt the kiss deep down to his heart and soul, and heat blossomed in his chest and radiated outward.

Obie let his hands wander, learning the contours of Bri's chest and shoulders. He already knew some of him from previous massages, but this was different. Then, he'd been doing his job; this was full-on, intense touch, and he wanted to memorize the curve of each muscle. He pulled back, burying his face in Bri's neck, inhaling as Bri stretched to give him access. He found a divot at the beginning of the shoulder, and worried it with his tongue, smiling as Bri quivered, groaning loudly.

"Good?" Obie breathed, trying to remain in control of himself. The energy and attraction frizzled between them, almost too much to process.

"Everywhere you touch me is good," Bri panted, and Obie grinned, going back to the task of drawing out as many whimpers and groans as possible. It was like a concerto of pleasure, the sounds mixing with his own to fill the room, building on each other until they echoed back to them over and over again. The crescendo came as Obie slowly slid down Bri's body, hands and tongue blazing a trail over his rippled belly before closing around Bri's length and taking it between his lips.

Bri's musky richness burst on Obie's tongue as he took him deeper. Obie was good at this, he knew it, and Bri did as well, in a matter of seconds. He lifted his gaze to Bri's and found half-hooded eyes, his mouth partially open, pure ecstasy emblazoned on his face. "I… oh my God…." Obie had reduced Bri to incoherence, and there was nothing sweeter. "Come here," Bri gasped. It was the first thing that made any sense, and Obie pulled away, letting Bri guide him to his lips. Their kiss seared the damn sheets, or at least it felt like it. Bri slid down the bed under him and guided Obie to turn around, straddling him. Then Obie lowered himself, gasping at the wet heat that surrounded him. He took Bri once more, letting the passion, lust, and pure ecstasy carry him away on winds of orgasmic wonder that seemed to go on forever.

Obie lay next to Bri a few minutes later, after his head cleared and he was able to think again. Sliding closer, he nestled right up to Bri, running his fingers lightly over his chest. "Wow."

"You can say that again," Bri whispered between breaths. "I could stay right here forever."

"That would be nice. We could keep the outside world at bay and not have to deal with anything." Of course, that wasn't realistic, but it was a nice thought. He closed his eyes and sighed, luxuriating in the way Bri's arm held him close and the heat that radiated off his body. The calming scent of cinnamon from the oil was a nice touch as well.

A DING from somewhere in the house pinged the edge of Obie's attention, just as he was falling to sleep. He ignored it until it came again. "I'll go see if I can find it," Obie said. He wasn't going to have Bri try to get out of bed.

"I think it's from somewhere close," Bri said, and Obie sighed, sliding off the bed and hoping it came again. After about a minute, it sounded once again and Obie followed it to the chair where clothes had been piled. He found Bri's pants and dug the phone out of his pocket, then handed it to Bri before joining him on the bed once again.

The light from the screen shone on Bri's face as he opened the message. He didn't seem to listen to it, but paled as he read. "What is it?" Obie leaned over, glancing at the transcript before locating his own phone. He pulled up his dad's number.

His father picked up on the second ring. "Dad, it's me. Bri got another message. It's a voicemail this time. Do you want to have someone come over here to pick it up or can it wait until tomorrow?" Obie groaned as he turned to the clock. He had a client coming before nine in the morning and he needed to rest at some point.

"I'll stop by in the morning on my way to the office," his dad said from the other end of the line. "Don't do anything to it, and I suggest you put the phone aside and leave it. Don't turn it off. But if this guy keeps calling, just let it go to voicemail and save everything."

"Thanks, Dad. I'll see you then." He hung up and relayed his dad's message to Bri. Then Obie took the phone, switched it to Vibrate, and set it inside one of his drawers before returning to bed. "Dad will come by to get it in the morning. And we should try to sleep. He's going to be here pretty early, and we don't want to look like we've been up all night."

"Okay." Bri didn't sound convinced, and Obie got up, pulled on his robe, and went back downstairs, checking that all the doors were locked and the windows shut tight. Then he came back up and climbed into bed.

"Dad will know what to do."

Bri nodded, and Obie doubted either of them was going to get much sleep. "I'm wondering if we should get your dad and my dad together on this one. They may be able to help each other out." Bri yawned, but Obie could sense that he was very much awake. He could almost feel the tension growing in his muscles.

"That's not a bad idea. Why don't we ask my dad in the morning? I'm sure he could use all the help he can get." Lord knew Bri needed the help and support. It was hard for Obie to understand what he was going through.

"And I'm thinking you may be right about my injury. I'll tell your dad about it in the morning and give him the name of the player. Maybe the guy can shed some light on this if the police apply enough pressure." Bri rolled onto his side and then back again, tossing and turning for a while.

"You know it's okay to be upset. No one wants to think that there's someone out there who wants to hurt him." He put an arm around Bri's chest. "Just relax and try to get some sleep. We can't let this asshole win, no matter what. You have to get ready to play again, and my dad and the police are going to find this freak and nail him to the wall."

Bri hummed. "Did you read the entire message?"

"No... I...." Obie paused.

"He threatened my friends. He's done it before, too," Bri whispered. "How can I keep them safe? What if he tries to burn their houses down? Or goes after their wives and kids? What am I supposed to do then?" He put his hands over his face. "I couldn't live with myself. It's bad enough he wants to hurt me, but.... What if he's decided that you or David or Chippy need to be the messengers—whatever the hell that means?"

Obie could almost feel Bri pulling away. "Don't you dare take this on yourself. Whatever this is about, we need to see if we can get to the bottom of it."

"I keep thinking this has to do with me being gay. He knows and hates it, because he keeps using the word 'abomination' in the messages. I mean, I know I've done some things more publicly lately, but I was pretty closeted before I hurt my knee. Hell, I never really had much time to do anything other than play, practice, and stay in shape for the next season." He held his head. "I keep going over things, and it's making my head hurt."

Obie gently lowered Bri's hands, massaging his temples and skull until some of the tension leached out of him. "Then let it go for now. Dad will get the message and then he can ask the questions he needs to. That word can have a lot of various meanings and uses, so let's not jump to conclusions." Obie grew quiet and slowly gentled his motions until Bri's eyes drifted closed and his breathing eventually evened out. Obie lay back down and did his best not to move, eventually falling into a fitful sleep, waking every few hours to check that Bri was okay and that the house was still quiet.

A BANGING woke him from the first sound sleep he'd gotten all night. The sheets were cold, and Obie was alone. He swore under his breath as he jumped out of bed, pulled on a robe, and hurried down the stairs, nearly tripping over his own feet. "Morning, James," he heard Bri say. By the time he reached the living room, his father and Bri were already choosing their chairs. "I made coffee," Bri said.

"I'll get it." God, he needed some strong stuff if he was to get his head working properly. His eyes felt gritty and he knew he looked like hell. Still, Bri smiled at him and made him shiver with that "starving man at a buffet" look. Obie padded into the kitchen, poured the coffee into mugs, and brought them in, passing them around.

Bri handed his dad his unlocked phone. "I didn't actually listen to the message last night, but I read the transcription. It was enough."

His dad nodded. "I'd like to take the phone and have my tech guys analyze it. We won't damage it, and I'll make sure you get it back, but we can clone it so we get any messages that are sent to you. We may be able to trace where this one came from." He sighed. "At least we can try. Everyone thinks it's pretty easy because they make it look that way on television, but it's anything but. Still, we may get lucky." He listened to the message with a scowl. Obie knew exactly what his father was thinking.

"He's escalating," Obie said, and his father nodded. "Whatever message he wants to get across, he thinks he's being clear about it, but he isn't really. It could be that his hold on reality is tenuous." Obie sat down, making sure his robe was closed. The last thing he wanted to do was flash his father.

"I agree with that," his dad said. "And that means that both of you need to be extra careful. I don't like the tone of these messages at all. They're threatening in the extreme and the net is being cast wider." He put the phone away and asked Bri for his unlock code. Bri wrote it down and handed it to him.

"I hate that this asshole has decided that my friends are fair game. What if he decides to go after my mom and dad? What sort of protection do they have?" Bri's hand shook again.

"His dad has mobility issues," Obie supplied.

"Yes. Dr. Early and I have worked together in the past. He's provided valuable insight to the department over the years."

"I was thinking that you might get him involved. He's already seen many of the notes, and like you said, he has insights that are different from the rest of ours." Obie finished his coffee and set the mug on the table, waiting for the caffeine to kick on. "Anyway, we appreciate you helping with this." Obie yawned and checked the time. He had a client coming in an hour and a half, and somehow he needed to be awake and functional, which probably meant a shower and three cups of coffee. "I know you need to get to work."

"Yes, I do." His dad finished his coffee. "Call if anything happens, and I'll let you know if we have anything concrete." He stood, and Obie walked him to the door, saying goodbye and locking it after him.

"I don't feel like I'm being brushed off, but I get the feeling that there isn't much they can do right now. It's as if we're waiting around for him to do something else. He wants something, but never says exactly what it is."

"Maybe the next time he calls, you should ask. We've been avoiding him, but why not ask him why he's doing this and what he wants? His answer, if he gives one, could be a clue to his motivation and ultimate identity. In police situations, Dad says the number-one thing to do is to try to get the perp talking. It often defuses the situation, and gives the police a chance to gather more evidence and catch the guy or get him to surrender." Obie wasn't sure how Bri would take that suggestion, but he figured he could give it a try.

"He seems to want to get his message across, whatever it is, so maybe he'll talk about it." Bri leaned back in the chair. "Of course, nothing is going to happen now until I get my phone back." He wasn't sure how he felt about being without it. Part of him felt naked and cut off from the world. Another part of him was glad he wouldn't have to worry about getting more calls. "I should get dressed and out of your hair."

Obie shook his head. "You should go back upstairs and try to get some sleep. I have a client, but you should keep that knee elevated. Let it rest, because we have an appointment tomorrow and you're going to need your strength." Obie winked and wished he could go back to bed too. But he had obligations and he wasn't going to let his other clients down. "It's also best if you stay out of sight."

"Okay." Bri got up, and Obie followed him up the stairs. He climbed back into bed, and Obie used the bathroom, shaved, and took care of business. By the time he came in to dress, Bri was sound asleep, snoring softly. Obie was quiet and got his things before returning to the bathroom, where he dressed, and then went downstairs, made a light breakfast, and got the therapy area set up and ready for his client. He yawned at least a dozen times during the process and drank another mug of coffee, knowing it was going to be a very long day. But the thought of Bri upstairs in his bed kept him going, as did the knowledge that neither of them knew where the inevitable next escalation would come.

"GOOD MORNING," Obie said to his new client as Clarice hobbled inside, half bent over and stiff. "Oh my goodness. Are you able to sit?" He grabbed a chair and brought it closer, adding a pillow. Clarice sat down, the pillow behind her back, a look of extreme relief washing over her. "Well, I think I have an idea of what's going on, but why don't you tell me?"

She sighed loudly, pain still evident around the edges of her face. "Business trip to the West Coast. Terrible plane seat, then a hotel bed from hell, sitting on terrible chairs in meetings, and by the time I could go home, I got off the plane like this. I've been given massage therapy and steroids that made me sick. I went to one of those large clinics where the therapist was much more interested in flirting with a coworker on the other side of the room than he was in me." Clarice winced in discomfort. "One of your former clients recommended you. He said you could help me and that you were a true professional. I don't expect to be the center of my therapist's world, but I do think I deserve his attention when I'm in an appointment, not to be treated as a distraction between phone calls." She shifted slightly, and a little more of the tension drained from her expression.

Obie handed Clarice the standard set of release and consent forms, as well as a medical history form, and let her fill them out, the entire time trying not to yawn and think about Bri upstairs in his bed. He had to keep his mind on his job and his client. Clarice deserved his entire attention. Once she was done, Obie reviewed the forms, made a few notes, and helped her onto the massage table so he could do whatever it took to enable Clarice to walk out of his session a little straighter and in less discomfort, than she'd come in. Too bad he couldn't say the same thing for himself.

CHAPTER 9

BRI FELT better after sleeping some more, but he had the strangest feeling that something wasn't right. He dressed as quickly as he could and got his brace on before grabbing his crutches and heading for the stairs. Voices drifted through from the back of the house, tickling the edges of his consciousness. "A woman...?" He couldn't quite hear what they were saying, but it bothered him. He went as far as the kitchen, poured himself a mug of coffee, and managed to make it to the table without spilling it.

He checked the time and wondered when Obie would be done. For the first time in weeks, he was surprisingly content. Sure, all this crap was happening, but he felt reasonably safe just knowing that Obie was here and that he wasn't alone. The worry was there, most definitely, but he could deal with it.

The door to the therapy room opened and closed and Obie dragged himself into the kitchen, pouring another cup of coffee before padding on through to the living room. Bri finished his drink and got the mug to the sink as the television flipped on and he heard the theme to *The Nanny*. God, he loved that show. It was on one of those rerun channels, and was his secret guilty pleasure. Especially the later episodes, where Maggie was dating the model and they had him shirtless a few times.

He went in, intending to join Obie on the sofa, but instead, he found him in the chair, half asleep, curled up almost into a ball. Bri stretched out on the sofa, half watching the television and keeping an eye on Obie, who wasn't watching him back. "Is something wrong?"

"No," Obie answered quietly as the commercial ended and the show began again. "I'm fine. Just tired." He said no more through the rest of the episode and into the next one.

"Okay. Something is bothering you." Bri sat up, carefully positioning his leg, wary and slightly on edge. "What's the deal?"

"I'm just thinking," Obie snapped. "Look, okay...." He unwound his legs. "What happened last night can't happen again, okay? I'm your therapist. I can't be your lover too. I know we've talked about this before, and last night I let my little head overrule my big head. But until you're on your feet again, we can't...." He waved his hand.

"So you want me to leave?" Bri asked. "I can go to a hotel, that's no problem." He used his crutches to get to his feet. "As long as I can use your phone... or is that unprofessional too?" He was pissed. Yeah, maybe he sounded like a kid, but this whole thing hurt. "You know I could just fire you." That was sounding more and more like a good idea.

"Yes, you could, but then who would be able to get you back to playing form? Remember, I'm, like, therapist number four." Obie sneered and then softened his expression. "Look, we just have to step back and remember that getting you healthy is what counts. You're getting stronger all the time, and soon you're not going to need that brace any longer. That's what we have to keep our eyes on. When you can play again."

Bri shook his head. "Are you really that selfless? Or just uncaring?"

"They say it in old movies all the time. If things are going to work out, then a few weeks of keeping our hands to ourselves isn't going to hurt us." He cocked his eyebrows, and Bri had to agree. But after last night, he wasn't sure he could do it, where Obie was concerned. He was like a drug and Bri was already addicted. "Just be patient so this doesn't feel like it's hanging over my head, that's all I'm asking. How would you feel if I wanted you to... I don't know, break some basketball player code of ethics? Like I wanted you to sleep with the center's wife?" He giggled, and Bri rolled his eyes.

"That's happened before—on my team, a few years ago. It was a mess."

"Well, then that's what I'm trying to avoid. I have to be professional and I'm already pushing it. So for now, we need to back away and let things cool down a little so I can do my job, and you can heal and get back to playing…. Then we can pick things up." Obie shivered. "I already have a hard time thinking of anything else but you. And I need to be detached. So when we're in the therapy room, it's you and me, Obie and Bri. No innuendo or stuff like that. We have to work and be professional." Obie sighed. "That doesn't mean you need to leave, but you should move into the guest room."

Bri nodded. He could see the conflict in Obie's expression and he hated that he'd been the one to put it there. Bri should have been smarter and thought about Obie and the position he was putting him in. "Okay. I agree things maybe moved a little fast because of the attraction and…." Bri's gaze caught Obie's, and damned if he didn't have to look away just because of the heat that sizzled right there. "I won't say that last night was a mistake. Never." Bri got to his feet. "I'm going to go get cleaned up and then make some calls, if I can use your phone." He needed to call the team and his agent, keep them up to date, and maybe talk to his dad. At the moment, though, he needed to get out of this room and give himself a moment to breathe without having Obie nearby. "Do you have another appointment?"

"In fifteen minutes," Obie said, and Bri nodded, leaving him to his work. "There's a wired line in the last room upstairs. I don't use it for much, but you can hook up the phone in there if you like. Go ahead and make all the calls you need."

"Thanks." Bri wanted to lean over Obie and kiss him breathless. The longer he stayed in the room, the better that idea sounded, so instead, he went upstairs and into a room that was lined with bookshelves and contained a single recliner and table. He plugged in the old rotary dial phone and sat still, realizing he didn't have the numbers he needed and no way to find them.

"I thought you might need this," Obie said, handing him a tablet. "We can have lunch when my appointment is over and then you and I can work for a while."

"Thanks. I really appreciate it." Bri called his father first, bringing him up to date, and then got in touch with the team manager.

"Are you okay?" Jack asked when Bri explained what had been going on. "I saw the news story. It's been running with each and every report. Thankfully you were smart enough not to give any interviews or talk to reporters. Have you contacted the police?"

"Of course. The father of a friend of mine is the police commissioner. He's been personally involved." That ought to shut Jack up. He could be a brilliant manager, but he sometimes had all the people skills of a tree stump.

"Is this friend… a *friend* friend?" Jack's attempt at subtlety was wasted. He was never subtle and most definitely out of practice.

"Look. I have decided that I am not going to talk about my personal life. If I want to have one, then it's my business." Bri sat back and prepared for battle. "I don't intend to give any sort of interviews on my personal life or talk about it with the media. And I have decided that I'm not going to talk about it with you or the team either. I play—that's what I get paid for, and I will be a part of this team again. My rehab is going well. But I will not answer those kinds of personal questions." He kept his voice firm.

"Your contract—"

"My contract is for my skills on the court, nothing more. I will not have the team telling me who I can see and what I can do. As I said, I won't answer any questions, so don't bother asking." He grinned as Jack began to sputter. He liked to know everything, and it was obviously getting under his skin big-time that Bri wasn't going to talk about this.

"On a more pertinent subject, I'm really making progress," Bri continued. "I can put weight on my leg and it's getting stronger. I also have more movement, and that's improving steadily too. In another month, I hope to be able to join the team for light workouts. I see the doctor in two weeks, and then we'll go from there." Keep it business. That was the one way to ensure that things remained professional.

"How is the pain?"

"Nonexistent right now. I get sore after therapy sessions, but that's about it. Like I said, I'm getting stronger and stronger." He paused. "Look, coach. I think I need to tell you that… the police will be looking into that incident on the court. Ever since then, I've been getting threats and… well, you know my house was set on fire, right? Someone has it in for me. Maybe the exhibition game was when it all started. It's probably a good idea for you to take a look at the videos yourself."

The other side of the line was silent for a long time. "You think it was deliberate?"

"It's possible. The police are on it. My friend's father, the police commissioner, thinks it's a strong possibility, so they aren't likely to let it go." Bri needed to let him know. "This should have been investigated a long time ago." He let the implication that this could hurt Jack professionally hang in the air.

"You know that's hard to determine. It was an exhibition game that got a little out of hand. The players got…." Jack groaned. "Do you have any idea the kind of trouble something like this is going to stir up? This sort of thing isn't done. What happens on the court stays there, and once the game is over, everyone shakes hands and goes home. It's how the game is played. You never know when you're going to end up on the same team as the guy who fouled you. That's life in this business. You know that." Bri had heard this lecture more than once. It was Jack's Professionalism Talk 101.

"This has nothing to do with that. Jack, what if someone purposefully set out to injure me? What if the injury and the threats, and someone setting my garage and car on fire, are all related? I know it's your job to think about the team, but part of my job is trying to stay alive and safe." He sighed and doubt began to creep into the back of his mind. "Do you even want me to come back? Or is all this some ploy to get me to leave the team?" Head offices played games all the damned time.

"Of course not. You're the heart of this team, and we need you back if we're going to have a shot at the title this year. But if we start going after players because of things that happen on the court, then—"

"I'm not. The police are interested." That was at least a way for him to stay one step removed. "I'm not pursuing it myself. But they have seen the footage and they're planning to do some follow-up. They'll probably want to talk to Young about what happened."

Jack swore under his breath. "I don't suppose that idiot will be smart enough to keep his mouth shut." Bri could almost see Jack shaking his head and pursing his lips as though he'd just sucked a lemon.

"It's not going to be easy, considering he's in New York, but we'll see what happens." There was little else he could do about it. "All I want is to get to the bottom of this so I can feel safe in my own home again, Jack. It's just getting to be too much. If there is some connection, then maybe once the police get to the bottom of it, I'll be able to get my life back." Damn it all, he hated sounding fucking whiny, and he knew that was exactly how it must seem. "Anyway, I wanted you to know what was going on. Don't interfere, though. Let the police do their job."

Jack was quiet once again. "All right. We'll let the police do what they need to, and I'll speak to management here and make sure the team is behind you." He sounded reluctant, and Bri wondered just how much effort he was going to put into this supposed support.

"Jack," Bri snapped. "I have never done anything to create trouble for the team. Never. I have played for years and always gave management the best I had. I'm the victim here, not the guy who burned down someone else's garage. Remember that." He was getting damned tired of this entire conversation. "I expected more support than this." Maybe he'd talk to his agent next, to see what kind of pressure he could add.

"This has the potential to put the team in a difficult position," Jack said.

"No, it doesn't. Either the team supports its players or it doesn't. Young isn't on the Rockets, but a rival team. So you should be standing behind me, because you know damn well the owner in New York is going to stick behind Young. It's one of the few things that Marv Kaufmann does right. He supports his people." Bri was laying it on thick, knowing that the other coach and Jack had an old rivalry. There was no way Jack was going to allow Marv to get the better of him.

"Okay. I see your point. God, I'm glad we have to deal with your agent at contract time, instead of you. After a few hours, I swear you'd end up as the owner of the entire team." He could see Jack rolling his eyes. "I'll do my best. But please be careful, stay healthy, and don't talk to the media. If it ever gets to that point, we'll work through what we're going to say."

"I'm surprised the media hasn't beaten a path to my door," Bri said.

Jack laughed. "That's because they don't know where you are, and I suggest you keep it that way." Bri breathed a sigh of relief. He had half expected to find a sea of reporters outside the house at any second. "You know what to do, and if there is any statement to be made—about anything—we will help you." He sounded genuine, and Bri agreed.

"I need to go. I have a therapy session coming up and I need to get something to eat first. I'll keep you in the loop."

"Okay," Jack agreed, and they ended the call. Bri set the phone in the cradle and stared at the picture of a vintage Mustang on the far wall without really seeing it. Even though Jack had said all the right things—well, he eventually had—Bri still wondered just how much Jack was on his side. Dammit, he needed to control his jitteriness. Not everyone was out to get him.

Footsteps outside the room, drawing closer, drew his attention. "I'm going to make some lunch. It's just sandwiches, but you can come down when you're done with your calls." Obie leaned against the doorpost, his arms hanging at his sides. In his tan slacks and blue polo shirt, he looked every bit the professional therapist, but those eyes, bright and as blue as the summer sky, gave Bri ideas he shouldn't be having after their earlier conversation.

"Is there anything else you need? I was thinking about making a call for dinner tonight and having something delivered." He wanted to make Obie happy and to thank him for letting him stay here.

"That would be nice."

"A friend of mine, Jacques, owns Le Jardin downtown. I'll see if he can put together one of his vegetarian specialties and arrange to have it delivered. He's done things like that in the past for me. Everything Jacques makes is incredible. You'll love it."

When Obie left, Bri picked up the phone once again, trying to get through the last of his calls. It would have been a lot easier if he hadn't known Obie was right downstairs the entire damned time.

BRI'S LEG ached, but in a good way. With Obie's help and a set of bars, he had been able to put most of his weight on his knee and walk slowly, without his brace. It felt amazing and was a real sign of progress. His insurance agent had received a copy of the preliminary reports about the fire and they were moving things forward. Jack had called him twice, as had his agent, and he had answered their questions. His agent was engaging a PR firm to handle any possible fallout and to field questions.

Obie was currently with another client, and Bri was just finishing up another round of calls, the last one to Obie's father. "We are trying to work out a way to speak to Mr. Young, but unfortunately, he has lawyered up and doesn't want to talk."

"Sounds guilty to me," Bri said. While Obie's dad didn't immediately agree with him, Bri got the feeling James thought the same thing.

"We only requested to speak with him, and he hid behind a lawyer mighty fast." James sounded frustrated. "It's okay, though. I've had some experts reviewing all of the videos and we're building enough of a case that we can press charges. Then he won't have much choice. Once we arrest him, he will answer our questions. It's only a matter of time." That made Bri feel somewhat better. "Justice doesn't always work quickly, but in the end, it usually works. Have there been any more messages or threats? We haven't received anything on your phone. By the way, I'll stop by in a few hours to return it to you."

"It's been really quiet, especially since you have my phone. I'm starting to think I should get rid of the thing and go off the grid. It would be easier all around." He was more relaxed and didn't jump every time the damned thing rang. "Part of me misses it, but the quiet has been nice."

"I understand," James said chuckling. "I have two of the infernal things and I want to throw each of them against the wall at least twice a day." A ringing in the background clued Bri in to exactly what he was talking about. "I have to go. Please tell Obie that I'll stop by." He hung up, and Bri set the phone down, pleased that he was done with his calls for a while. Movement below told him that Obie was finished, and he made his way down the stairs, finding Obie in the kitchen.

"What are you doing? I have dinner covered," Bri said as Obie fussed.

"I know. I need something to do."

"Your dad is going to stop on his way home," Bri told him, which only sent Obie into another flurry of activity. "Why do you do that? Your dad can see the house as it really is. Hell, the place is damned near spotless, but if your dad says he's coming over, you run around fluffing the pillows to within an inch of their lives and worrying about a stray dust bunny under the sofa that no one is going to see unless they get down on their hands and knees. And I don't see that happening."

"I get so nervous sometimes." Obie began wiping down the already-gleaming counters and then set the rag aside to grab a broom to sweep the polished floors. "Don't you ever wonder?" He swept like the devil himself was after him. "If you were a disappointment? I do sometimes. My dad loves the outdoors and goes hunting up north on his vacations. He took me camping twice. The first time, I screamed when bugs got in the tent, and wanted to sleep in the car. The second time, I was with my dad in a deer blind and he was going to help me shoot my first deer. All I did was cry, saying that Dad was going to shoot Bambi's mother, and refused to stop. I think I was eleven. At least we both love sports and were able to go to games together. I wasn't a total disappointment, but Dad had been the quarterback in high school, and I was never going to make any team other than debate."

"Your dad is proud of you, I'm sure of it. If he isn't, then he isn't worthy of having a son like you. Okay?" Bri stopped the swish of the broom, stilling it. "Each and every son worries about disappointing his father at some point in their lives. But you are not your dad and he isn't you. Obie is an individual, and I like the man that Obie is. He's kind and strong and independent. He cares for others, but is also willing to be taken care of." Bri nodded slowly. "Obie is someone worth being proud of."

Obie's eyes shone, and Bri set his crutches aside and took him in his arms, gingerly balancing on his injured leg. "Don't hurt yourself," Obie mumbled as Bri cradled his shoulders and head against his chest.

"And stop feeling guilty for being the man you are," Bri reiterated. "We all have things we regret," he added in a whisper.

"What do you regret?" Obie asked and Bri closed his eyes.

"Willy Hamel," he said softly, opening that last little door in the back of his mind. This was the second time he'd thought about him in the last few weeks. He'd come to mind when Obie had told him about what had happened to his friend Harper. And suddenly, the memories came flooding back. "Willy." He held Obie tighter as he stood silently, wishing he could go back and change the past.

"Why?" Obie asked, closing his arms around his waist. "Did you hurt him?"

Bri shook his head. "No... yes... I don't know." He shook as he tried to find the words. "I was a freshman in college and thought I knew everything, though I didn't know shit about shit. Willy was a freshman too. He had a room down at the other end of the hall in the same dorm as me. One of my teammates was his roommate." He swallowed around the lump. "Darryl tormented Willy no end. He didn't know why he had to share a room with Willy and wanted him moved. The campus was crammed full and there was no space, so both he and Willy were stuck. Then Darryl took it on himself to drive the kid away, and got other team members to help. It was awful. And I did nothing," Bri said. "Nothing at all. I was too damned scared." He turned away, looking at the kitchen wall with its large clock.

"I take it Willy was gay," Obie said.

139

Bri shrugged. "I don't know. I guess the term today would be pansexual or polysexual. He was just another guy trying to figure out who he was, and Darryl made his life hell. Willy was on medication that made him sleep heavily, so one night, they carried his mattress out of the room and left him outside—in the rain." Bri shook his head. "It got to the point that I remember Willy sitting up most of the night in the common room because he was too afraid to go to his own, terrified of what Darryl and his friends would do to him. And I simply stood by, watching, and let it happen." Bri wiped his eyes.

"This doesn't sound like it ends happily," Obie said quietly, as though half holding his breath.

Bri shook his head. "That depends. I remember talking with Willy in the common room. He was practically living there at one point. He told me he had put in for another transfer, and this time, housing had told him that they'd found him a new room. He was happy and relieved." Bri groaned softly. "I should have just invited him to come stay with me for a few days. My roommate and I had a sofa under our loft beds and he could have slept there until he had his own place. At least then he would have been safe. But no… I was too scared." He sighed. "Willy knew Darryl's schedule and used to go back to sleep when he was away. Only he didn't wake up once, and Darryl went too far. Willy was allergic to lavender. When Darryl found out, he brought one of those scented plug-ins into the room and set it up near Willy's bed while he was asleep." Bri quivered.

"Oh God…," Obie said.

"Yeah. I remember the ambulance, the sirens, everyone standing in the hallway watching as Willy was carried out of the room. He was alive and had one of those breathing masks on, but his eyes were closed and he was still, really still. Someone must have called his family, because his mom, dad, and older brother were there by the time they got him into the ambulance, huddled together in the dorm lobby." Bri released Obie and turned away, sitting back at the table. "Everyone says you regret what you didn't do, sometimes more than your own actions."

"Did he live? Was he okay?"

Bri nodded. "He lived. But they said that it had severely damaged his lungs. Willy never came back to school again." He turned away. "The shitty thing was, I was like Willy. I had a similar secret—well, he wasn't so secret—but I was afraid to help him because I didn't want anyone to know about me and I was… a coward." He sat down. "I'm still a fucking coward." He held his head and stared at the floor. "I hide who I am from most everyone. I have few friends, real friends, and those I do have, I'm scared to be around too much because they're gay and open about it." He hung his head.

"Bri, I don't think things are that bad, and—"

"Yes, they are. I've let fear make most of my life decisions for me. I stayed quiet when Willy was hurt and I could have done something. I avoid doing things that might make people guess at my secret. I tell myself that I don't hide it, but I really do. The only thing I've ever done to be brave and open was to go to that club, and I only did that because I was with friends and they would tell everyone that I was only there to support a good cause. They covered for me so I could once again be a coward." He sighed. "I have to stop this." He stood, his leg shaking, and he nearly went down, but Obie grabbed him and helped Bri get his balance once again.

"Hey, you brought me and the guys to the game and came to my rescue when you thought someone was going to hurt me." Obie stood behind him, hands placed gently on his shoulders. "Everyone needs to come to grips with who they are in their own time. I firmly believe that."

A knock interrupted them, and Obie's hands slipped off his shoulders. He left the room, and Bri swiped his hands over his face, trying to smooth away the sick feeling in his gut. "Thank you," Obie said, his voice drifting in from the other room. "Yes, I have the instructions. Thanks again." The door closed, and Obie returned with a large bag. "Dinner."

Bri nodded, though he wasn't very hungry right now. Obie set the bag on the counter. "We're supposed to put this in the oven for half an hour at 350, so I'm going to do that now."

"Okay," he agreed passively. Bri didn't have the energy for anything right now. His mind kept going over his decisions of the last ten years of his life. Nearly every one of them had been made to keep his secret, to hide who he was. And it had been Obie, even without him realizing it, who had changed the way he acted. With Obie, he made decisions that he wanted to make and his secret became less important. So he was a gay basketball player? So what? Did that mean he didn't deserve to have a life that made him happy, that he was to live without love? Bri shook his head slowly. God, he had been stupid for leading half a life all these years. "What am I going to do?"

Obie closed the oven door. "About what?"

"Everything." Bri wanted to close his eyes and pretend he could hide from this. He'd been hiding from who he was and what he really wanted for so long, he barely understood how to do anything else. But that had to end—soon.

"No." Obie put the rest of the food in the refrigerator and closed the door. "I think you expect this to be some big event, something you have to orchestrate. It isn't. This is about living your life authentically. There doesn't have to be any media attention at all if you don't want there to be. Just be who you are." Obie pulled out the chair next to him and sat down.

"But I live part of my life in the public eye. I have to think about what will happen when this comes out." Bri sat up straighter and laughed because he could do nothing else.

Obie shook his head and smiled. "It's just about you being you. If you want to tell your manager and agent, go ahead. Tell the team, if you wish, but then let the chips fall where they may. Just let yourself be you." He took Bri's hand. "I think that's what you've been missing." Obie smiled at him, his eyes lighting just a little.

"What's that for?"

"I always smile when I look at you." Obie squeezed his hand a little tighter. "It takes courage to be who we really are. Do you remember high school and the guy who was always so filled with confidence? The guy who walked into a room and radiated charisma and made you want to look at him? Was he a lie, or was he the guy who was being who he was and was lucky enough that he fit in with what everyone expected? Anyway, looking at you makes me happy, so I do it as often as I can."

Bri sighed and straightened his shoulders. He wasn't going to let this—or anything else—get him down if he could help it. Obie was right. He needed to be who he was and to hell with everyone else. "Once all this crap is over, and the asshole who keeps threatening me is behind bars, I'll talk to everyone." That was the only way he was ever going to be happy.

The scent of dinner wafted out of the oven, filling the room. "This is not how I wanted this to go. I had planned a nice dinner that we could enjoy, not…." What the hell did he call the nightmarish trip down memory lane he'd taken for the last hour? Bri pushed out a huge breath and stood. "I'll help you set the table." It was time to try to put some of this out of his head, at least for now.

He got up and used one crutch to steady himself as he got the silverware, setting it on the table, and then got the plates. Obie pulled the food out of the refrigerator and set out the serving containers, minus their lids. The salads looked amazing, and rich smells filled the kitchen.

By the time Obie pulled the dish out of the oven, the room smelled heavenly. "Ratatouille, I love it." Obie grinned as he set the hot dish on a cork trivet in the center of the table, adding a serving spoon. "Go ahead and sit. I'm going to get a bottle of wine. This is too good not to celebrate." Obie hurried away, returning with two glasses. He opened the bottle, poured glasses, and sat next to Bri, bumping his shoulder. "Thank you for this. It's really special."

Bri found it difficult to take his eyes off Obie, even for the incredible dinner. He wanted to be able to look at him—at his incredible eyes and intensely red hair—forever. He leaned closer, as Obie followed, kissing him, his hand sliding around to cup the back of Obie's head. He tasted his sweet lips, the perfect aperitif, before drawing back. He had made a promise to take things slower and he was going to keep it, no matter how much he wanted more.

OBIE GROANED as he sat back in his chair. "That was something else," he moaned softly, his hands rubbing his belly. "Jacques is some friend."

"He's really talented. He started Le Jardin a few years ago and has been struggling to make a go of it. His reviews have been good, but it's taken some time for him to get a real following and regular customers. It's starting now, and most nights he's nearly full. I'm happy for him. And you can tell by the food that it's definitely worth it."

"Oh yeah." Obie closed his eyes.

"There's dessert too," Bri offered. "Though I'm sure it has dairy in it." Berries and chocolate cream with a touch of brandy. It was something Bri loved but didn't get very often, especially when he was in training, which was most of the time.

"I don't think I can eat anything else right now. Maybe in a little while." Obie slid open those magnificent eyes, and Bri watched him, loving the way Obie licked his lower lip as though his tongue was searching for more of the heavenly goodness, but was coming back a little disappointed each time.

"All right. But it shouldn't sit too long. It's best when fresh." Bri stood and slowly cleared the dishes. He hated what a pain in the butt it was to do some of the simplest things.

"You can start using your leg without the crutches. You're strong enough, as long as you're careful," Obie said. "Just use the crutches when you're out or going up and down stairs. Check with the doctor if you want to make sure."

Bri tested it carefully. There was no pain, and he was able to use both hands. It was almost a miracle—at least it felt that way. He put the dishes in the sink and the remaining food into the refrigerator.

"You know, I could get used to this," Obie said slipping his hands behind his head, a wry grin on his lips.

Bri ran his fingers along Obie's ribs and he giggled as his arms came down to protect sensitive areas from Bri's tickling fingers. "You could, huh?" Bri grinned and relented. He didn't want Obie to wriggle his way out of the chair and onto the floor.

"Yeah, I could. You arranging dinner was very nice." Obie's laughter subsided and he got to his feet. "Let's go in the other room." He led the way, and Bri carefully followed, sitting on the sofa and putting his leg up. "We could watch television," Obie offered, as a knock sounded. Then the front door opened and the decision was made for them.

"Hey, Dad," Obie said as he jumped to his feet.

"I brought Bri back his phone." He came over and handed it to Bri. "I also wanted to ask a few more questions. We were able to speak with Young and we did some checking into his background. It wasn't hard. It seems Young is in debt up to his ears because he likes to play the horses."

"Did he admit to hurting me on purpose?" Bri asked.

James nodded. "The NYPD was very helpful and they did some checking. They found a ten-thousand-dollar deposit a week before you were injured. It didn't take much to make him think we knew more than we did and he caved pretty quickly. Yeah, he took the money, and all he had to do was make sure you got hurt. What we don't know is why."

"Did he say who paid him?" Obie asked, sitting next to him and taking his hand in support.

"No. I don't think he knows. He was desperate for money and was willing to sell his professional soul. We'll notify the league. He's been charged and is under arrest. The charges aren't all we could level, but that was part of the deal for the information."

"Okay." Bri's head spun. "So, where do we go from here?" It seemed they took one step forward and then hit another wall.

"That's what I wanted to talk to you about. Who would hate you enough to pay ten thousand dollars to hurt you?" James leaned forward in his chair.

"I don't know." He turned to Obie. "It isn't like I go around pissing people off all the time."

"No. But you have a reputation for being stubborn and demanding sometimes. Though I doubt that's why. There's professional jealousy, of course. That Donald guy comes to mind. He's a real piece of work."

"You mentioned him to the officers, and we looked into it. There's no evidence to prove that the money came from him. And you said it wasn't his voice. While I'm not discounting it, I think this is more than that. This is downright hate. Someone's door is a little off its hinges, and for whatever reason, they blame you." James sighed.

"Tell Dad what you told me before dinner," Obie said.

"That was freshman year," Bri countered. "And I never hurt him. I just feel bad because I never stopped it." He wished he'd kept his big mouth shut.

"Why don't you tell me," James said.

"Because it can't have anything to do with this," Bri said. "And…." Damn it all. He hated revealing shit like this about himself. He turned to Obie, almost not able to believe that he'd betrayed him that way.

"It's okay. Dad isn't going to judge you. Just tell him what you've told me. It may help. We don't really know, and he needs all the facts. I know it's hard, but no one can help if they don't know the facts. He wants to help, and so do I," Obie added just above a whisper.

Bri couldn't argue with those beseeching eyes, and reminded himself that he wanted to have courage and this was part of it. Girding his loins, so to speak, he told James what had happened and why he felt guilty. James listened without asking questions until the end. "What was Willy's full name? Can you remember?"

"William Hamel. He was from Johnstown. I remember that. I think he went there. I know he never returned to school." Bri lowered his gaze. "I probably should have asked after him."

James nodded, and when Bri raised his gaze, he found James staring at him. "Did you like Willy? In the way you like my son?"

Bri swallowed and nodded. "I think that's why I kept watching him. But I was afraid to say anything or act on it."

"Let me ask you this. Do you think Willy blamed you for what happened?" James asked, his eyes reminding Bri of Obie's in some ways. Bri kept expecting judgment, but saw compassion and understanding.

"How could he? I know this is guilt on my part. I wish I had been strong enough to do something about it. There are plenty of

146

stories—books are full of them—of people doing the right thing to help someone else. I wish I'd had the guts to try then. That's all."

Obie patted his hand. "You aren't alone," James said. "I have done many things in my life that I'm not proud of. It's what we do when we're young. Let me look further into this and see if it leads anywhere. I'll also check out your other teammates as well. It can't hurt." He paused. "I've looked into the people close to you and found nothing. There is no one truly suspicious, which makes me nervous."

"Why, Dad?" Obie asked.

"Most hatred comes from people that we have contact with regularly, ones we have a chance to hurt, a buildup of animosity that festers over time. That's why we look at the family first when anyone is murdered. Like on television, husbands and wives are the usual killers, as are children and even parents. But I haven't found anything. So I'm casting a wider net."

"What about that girl you told me about?" Obie said. "You said she always blamed you. Why don't you tell Dad about what happened back then too?"

James sat back, and Obie hurried away, returning with a tray and mugs of coffee. Bri figured what the hell and told James every one of the stories he'd imparted to Obie. It felt like airing years of dirty laundry and shame. Bri wondered what James thought of him by the time he was done.

"Is there anything else you can think of?" James asked as he consulted his notes and then drank the last of the coffee.

"No. Unless I have a stalker who's just found out some things he or she didn't like," Bri offered.

"That is a possibility. But it complicates things a great deal. Of course, if you see anyone acting funny around you, or feel as though you're being watched, call right away. Don't confront them yourselves. This person has already proven themselves capable of doing some major damage."

"We know, Dad. We're just waiting for the other shoe to drop. Did you get anything off the phone?"

"We're still working on it. If you receive any phone calls, let us know immediately, preferably while they are on the line. We have cloned it and hope we can get some information out of it."

"But you said that's a long shot, right?" Obie asked, and James nodded as Bri's phone rang. He stiffened and looked at it, catching James's gaze before answering. But when he picked up, there was no one there. At least the line was active, but after saying hello a couple of times and getting no answer, he hung up.

"That was interesting." Bri explained and handed the phone to James. The number didn't match any that had called before. "I get calls occasionally from telemarketers with those damned clicks that let you know the call is automated. It could be one of those."

"Possibly, but they usually have someone come on the line if you wait." James handed the phone back. "We'll have a record of the call. Just be careful, and if he contacts you, let me know right away. We'll try to trace the call while it's active. So keep him talking if you can and ask why he's doing this. What did you ever do to him? Those sorts of questions. We may get a nugget of information that we can use. There is also the possibility that he wants to talk."

Bri didn't think that was particularly probable, but he didn't argue. "I'll do my best."

"Of course we will, Pop," Obie said.

"I could put someone here in the house to keep an eye on both of you," James offered again.

Obie hesitated, but Bri wasn't sure it was a good idea. "Someone else who will draw attention to us. Right now, very few people know where I am, and I'd like to keep it that way. I think Obie and I are safest if I just remain out of sight."

"All right, but be careful. If I knew what this person wanted, I'd counter it, but I'm at a loss. All we know is that he or she wants to hurt you." James got up, and Obie did the same, slowly walking with him to the door.

"We'll be okay, Dad. I have my gun upstairs and I know how to use it. You made sure of that," Obie said. Bri didn't know if that soothed his dad or made him even more nervous. "So don't worry about us. We can take care of ourselves." He opened the door, and Bri stayed back, letting the two of them say goodbye. Once Obie closed the door, he sighed and started cleaning up the dishes.

"A gun…?" Bri asked.

Obie turned as though Bri had just asked the dumbest question possible. "I am the son of the police commissioner, a cop who has seen everything low and dirty this city can churn out. As soon as I graduated from high school, Dad took me to a gun range, taught me how to shoot, and drilled everything he knew into my head about safety, storage, cleaning, and usage of a gun. He made sure I was a damn good shot and then he bought me a Luger. I am deadly accurate with it and go to the gun range once a month to ensure I stay that way." His eyes held a darkness Bri had never seen in them before, and he wasn't sure if it scared him or turned him on. "I'm going to be safe in my own home." Obie went back to finishing up the dishes, got the dishwasher running, and then poured Bri another coffee. "It's decaf, so you'll be able to sleep."

"Did your dad know that?"

Obie shook his head. "God, no. Dad drinks this godawful stuff that I swear can stand on its own. It's awful, but he exists on it half the time. So when he comes here, I make good coffee, decaf, and he thinks it's great. And tonight, he isn't going to be up half the night."

"You're sneaky."

"Yes, probably, but I worry about him. He spends way too much time at work and he doesn't take any time for himself. Lord knows the last time he had a date. I wish he would do something, anything, for himself. But he says he's happy…." Obie rolled his eyes dramatically. "I just want him to take better care of himself."

"Your dad is an adult and he can take care of himself, I'm sure." Bri winked. "Besides, how do you know he doesn't have a string of lady friends? It isn't like your dad is likely to tell you about his bedroom activities… unless he gets serious about someone."

Obie screwed his face up in distaste. "I want Dad to be happy, but I don't want to hear about his bedroom prowess." He shivered, and Bri grinned at the melodrama. Obie could make him smile, that was for certain. "Why don't we see if we can find something frivolous to watch on television."

Bri nodded and checked his phone. There was a message about a team meeting the following morning, and another one from the insurance adjuster wanting to meet at the house. "What time is your first appointment?"

"Eight. I have an early one," Obie answered with a yawn. They got up and settled together on the sofa. They ended up watching *Big Bang Theory* reruns with Obie leaning against him and Bri eventually extending his arm around him, just like in high school. It was nice, and each time he inhaled, Bri got a strong whiff of Obie's sweet yet musky scent, which drove him crazy and pushed at the boundaries of his self-restraint.

"I should go on up to bed," Bri said softly as his control dipped to a low ebb. He was seconds from pushing Obie back against the cushions and tasting the man in every way possible. Instead, he got to his feet—a little unsteadily—and, using his crutches, went up to bed, wishing he wasn't going to be alone.

"I SAW him with that man again!" I smile in delight. This could be good. *Really* good. "Maybe I can take them both out at the same time. I'll make Bri watch as his lover fades away. Then he'll be sorry."

CHAPTER 10

OBIE WOKE three or four times in the night, just like he had for the last three nights. Most of the time, he lay awake, staring at the ceiling, trying to get to sleep, but ended up getting up to have some water or use the bathroom. Eventually he fell asleep, only to wake up a few hours later. Sometimes, he had no idea what woke him, but then he'd hear the creak of one of the floorboards in the hall and he knew Bri was up and awake. Then his body went on alert, and he listened as Bri closed the bathroom door. He actually wondered if he should wander out, but rolled over instead and tried to go back to sleep. It was his idea to take things slow and be professional in his dealings with Bri. Sometimes he really was a stupid ass. Obie sighed. He'd made his bed and now he had to lie in it… alone.

After rolling over, he fell asleep at some point, waking at first light feeling as though he'd been run over by a steamroller. Getting out of bed, he yawned and groaned when he stretched. Maybe he needed to take some of his own advice and spend more time getting his own body in order. Once he dressed, Obie went down to the studio, laid a mat on the floor, and spent some time stretching and doing some mind- and body-centering yoga. He needed to put Bri out of his head for a while and try to find some kind of inner peace.

It was elusive. His head and body did not want to go in the same direction. Or maybe it was his head and heart that were at war. Obie stretched his back and legs, shifting into a downward dog pose, holding it and breathing deeply. It wasn't working—nothing was.

"I made a light breakfast," Bri said. Obie lowered his body only to find Bri staring at him from the doorway. He stifled a groan at the heat in Bri's gaze and reached for his towel. "And I called for a driver to come pick me up," Bri continued. "The adjuster has finally decided to show up today. I need to be at the house in an hour." Obie must have been wet, and he didn't move as Bri took the towel and wiped off his cheeks and the back of his neck.

"I have appointments, so I can't go with you."

"I'll be fine. The driver doesn't know who I am, and he may recognize me, but…." Bri shrugged. "I'll get home, meet this guy, and then come back. It shouldn't be a particularly big deal."

Obie didn't like it. "Are you sure this guy is for real?" The thought that there was someone out there who wanted to hurt Bri was always foremost in his mind.

"I'll be okay. And I should be back in plenty of time for our appointment this afternoon. Come get some breakfast, and then you can clean up in time for your first client." Bri waited for him to leave the studio and followed him to the kitchen.

"Are you watching my butt?" Obie asked, whirling around and catching Bri in the act. "You are…." He wiggled it back and forth. "May as well give you something really good to look at." He laughed as he twerked, nearly falling over as Bri growled from behind him. Obie barely made it to the kitchen standing up, flopping into one of the chairs, laughing. Bri sat down, scowling at him, and Obie laughed harder. "What?" For some reason, this whole thing hit him as funny. It was either that or scream in frustration. Yes, this had been his idea, but it wasn't working out very well.

"You're not being nice."

"I know, I'm sorry." He got control of himself. "I haven't slept well for the last few days and I think I'm a little punch-drunk." He breathed deeply and took a piece of toast from the plate. "When will your car be here?"

"Ten minutes," Bri answered curtly.

"Hey, I wasn't trying to hurt you."

Bri set down his mug with a thud. "This shit is hard," he said softly. "You're in the next room, and I know I promised and all, but it's hard knowing you're there and that I need to keep my hands—and everything else—to myself."

"It's only for a few more weeks. By then, your knee is going to be in great shape and you're not going to need me anymore."

"I don't think that's true," Bri said in a gruff whisper that hung in the air around him. "I have the feeling that I'm going to need you for quite a while." His half-lidded eyes were banked with fire. It sent a wave of heat through Obie, and he swallowed his toast, gulping a mouthful of juice as he looked at the clock.

"I need to get ready for my next appointment," Obie said, ready to race out of the room.

"Can I have a kiss?" Bri asked, trying to look innocent. Obie paused and turned back, approaching Bri and leaning down. Bri slipped his hot, slightly rough hands around the back of Obie's neck, tugging him down into a kiss that damn near buckled Obie's knees. He gave himself over to it, ready to say "what the hell" and just go with whatever Bri wanted. His mind clouded with lust and aching need, and his willpower hung on by a thread. Bri backed away first. "You should get ready for your client." He slipped his hand away, running his fingers over Obie's cheek, slowly, gently, teasing out the touch the way he'd tugged his lips before finally pulling away.

Obie couldn't move for a second, blinking, his mind short-circuiting. "Yeah." He licked his lips, and Bri stood.

"My car will be here in just a minute."

Obie nodded, watching breathlessly as Bri grabbed his keys and wallet and slowly moved to the front door. Only when it closed did Obie grasp the back of the nearest chair, his chest heaving, swearing under his breath that he had to be the dumbest person on the face of the earth. He had a man like Bri, sex on a tall, muscular, hot-as-hell stick, and he was holding him at arm's length because of… "Professional ethics," Obie said out loud. He wasn't a doctor, but he was in the health-care profession, and it was important to maintain a professional distance. He had already crossed the line, but he didn't want to stray too far. Otherwise he was going to have to refer Bri to another therapist. And not to blow his own horn, but he was the best. After all, Bri was getting so much better.

He hurried upstairs and sat on the edge of the bed, checking the time once again. He figured he had ten minutes, so he picked up the phone. "Chippy, I need your help," he said as soon as his friend answered.

"Sounds serious," Chippy said without any of his usual flippancy.

"It is." He told him about what he and Bri had done and what he was afraid of. "I know what you and David said before, but this is serious."

"Okay. I could give you all the shit in the world over this one, but in all seriousness, I think the oldest advice is the best. If you wait until he's healed, and things are still hot between you, then go for it, full-on, no holds barred. Take the man to heaven and back as many times as you can. Do your best imitation of rabbits. But waiting isn't going to kill either one of you. And before you ask, if he won't wait, then he isn't worth your time." Chippy was so serious, Obie didn't know what to think. He kept expecting a joke to follow. "Stop worrying. He looks at you like you're a casino buffet and he walked ten miles to get there."

"I know. But it seems sort of stupid to wait when it seems like something we both want," Obie said.

"Okay. So what if he becomes your lover, and your client, and you have to give him bad news—is it going to be easier? Will you be distracted? Well, more than you already are. I'd say you're already in a relationship with this man and that you should probably back away now, except he needs you." Leave it to Chippy to lay it all out in black and white. "Be careful and go slowly. Give both of you some time. You've already got the man living with you."

"That's temporary," Obie protested, probably too rapidly.

"I know it is. But you've been in each other's pockets for a while, and things are bound to get muddled up. A little distance is good. It'll give you a chance to think. How long is he going to be there?"

Obie sighed, knowing Chippy was right. "A few more days. Bri was meeting the adjuster this morning, and he has already hired a restoration company to start getting the smoke smell out of the house." He wasn't sure how happy he was about the whole thing, but Chippy was right. Distance and going back to a more normal type of relationship would probably do them both good. "Thanks for the help."

"I hate to throw a wet blanket...."

"You didn't tell me anything I didn't already know." He checked the clock. "I have to go. I have a client soon and then a really full day. Two new clients are coming in, so it's going to be busy." He thanked Chippy and hung up, making a beeline for the bathroom to clean up and get ready to start his day.

GOD, HE was hungry. Obie had worked all morning. And with a few appointments running behind, he hadn't had enough time to stop for much more than a drink of water. Still, Mr. Cavendish was on his way out, and he expected the first of his new clients any second.

The back gate opened as Obie downed a glass of juice, settling his stomach a little before he opened the back door to let the man in. "Mr. Kelvin," Obie said with a smile, extending his hand. "I'm Obie Kenoble. It's good to meet you." They shook hands rather lightly and Obie motioned him inside. He got the forms and then went over them.

"Call me Harvey," his new client said as they talked about his back issues.

"I believe I can help you. I'm going to have you take off your shirt and get up on the massage table. I want to get an exact idea of where the pain is." He turned his back to give him a chance to get ready. "Do you need help?" Obie groaned as his phone rang. He ignored it and it rang again. "Will you excuse me?" Obie hated to interrupt a client, but he was only going to be a moment. He reached his phone in the kitchen just as it stopped ringing. He checked his call record. It had been his dad. He glanced at his messages as he returned to the therapy room, where Harvey was on the phone.

"I'm here right now. So you better listen to me closely...." Harvey turned to him as soon as Obie entered. He recognized the voice now, but it was too late. Harvey leaped out of the chair with no apparent back issues at all. And before Obie could react, he was down on the floor.

Obie struggled and nearly got free from Harvey. "Now you need to settle down, or I'll twist that pretty neck of yours and then that will be the end of you," Harvey snarled, and Obie stilled. He had no choice, especially with the way Harvey gripped him. Obie had been overpowered. He glanced from side to side to see if there was anything he could use as a weapon, but, pinned to the floor, he had no way of reaching anything.

"All right."

A rag pressed over his nose, and Obie did his best to breathe through his mouth, but it did no good. He became light-headed and slumped to the floor, closing his eyes as blackness threatened to overtake him.

OBIE BLINKED and didn't move. The cloth was gone from his nose and he wondered how long he'd been fogged out. It couldn't have been long. He wasn't tied, but he was still lying on the floor. Harvey was somewhere behind him, nervously pacing the floor. "Where is he? I should have known. He's no better now than he was then, the bastard." He stopped and came closer. Obie closed his eyes and kept his breathing level, even though his heart raced a mile a minute.

Hopefully Bri had called his dad once he'd talked with Harvey, though Obie had no idea. Obviously, Harvey expected Bri to come to meet him.

"Okay, little guy." Harvey slipped his arms under him, lifting Obie up. "It's time you and I go for a ride." As soon as he was off the floor, but before Harvey straightened up, Obie jerked, thrashing in Harvey's arms and going for his face, gouging at his eyes.

Harvey dropped him as he tried to protect himself, and Obie scrambled to his feet, racing out of the room, through the house and toward the front door. He heard Harvey bearing down on him, but managed to get the door open and leap out, slamming it behind him as a car pulled up. "Obie!" Bri called as sirens sounded, getting closer. "Get in!" Bri opened the door, and Obie dove into the back seat, tugging the door closed. "Go!" Bri told the driver and he took off.

"Did you call Dad?"

"Yes. He's on his way," Bri said and then told the driver to go around the block. Sure enough, by the time they reached the front of the house again, police cars had blocked the street. He had the driver pull over, and Bri paid him before they got out.

Obie approached the nearest officer. "This is my house," Obie said, even as his father strode through the line and right up to him, hugging him tightly.

"Are you okay? Did he hurt you?" his dad asked.

"He tried. Had something like chloroform in a rag. He put it over my nose, but I did what you told me to. I breathed through my mouth and then held my breath. He thought I had passed out. I was groggy—and now I have a headache—but I recovered quicker than he thought and surprised him."

"There's no one in the house now, sir," an officer said.

"He was mainly in the studio," Obie told his father. "He probably left plenty of evidence. He wasn't trying to hide his tracks. Check the massage table, and I can show you some things he touched," Obie offered.

"Okay, but don't touch anything yourself." He led the way inside, and Obie showed them the clipboard that still had the guy's intake form on it, as well as the pen he'd used. He also pointed out the other things Harvey had touched before leaving the room.

Obie was able to describe his attacker in great detail. "He can't be very far away. Bri had already called you, and I wasn't out more than maybe ten minutes… tops." Obie left the house and joined Bri on the sidewalk as the police did their jobs. He answered all their questions to the best of his ability, and no, he didn't want to go to the hospital. He was going to be fine and only had a slight headache, which was dissipating. Other than that, he wasn't hurt…. He hadn't recognized the man and had no idea if the name he had was the guy's real one or not. Questions followed questions until Obie was exhausted. The police finally finished inside.

"You need to stay somewhere else. Harvey Kelvin knows where you are—both of you, I suspect. Now, I want you to come stay with me for a few days. We'll track this guy down, and then you can return home."

Obie groaned. "What am I supposed to do about my clients, my job? Just leave them hanging? I can't, Dad, you know that. They rely on me, and letting them down is out of the question. You can station an officer here if you like, but I won't be driven out of my own house by some crackpot." He put his arms over his chest, defying his father to argue with him. "You know I can be just as stubborn as you are." And he could. Lord knew he'd learned from the best.

"I do." His dad turned to Bri. "Are you okay with this? We can put you up in a hotel and provide you with protection until we find this man."

"Obie," Bri said. "Why don't we stay here during the day so you can keep your appointments, but go to a hotel at night? That way we can be safe and sleep better without worrying. I can make a few calls and get us a room at a really nice place." He already had his phone out, but didn't actually call until Obie nodded. It made sense, and they needed to be safe. "You can have someone here during the day," Bri told James. "As long as Obie is okay with it."

Obie nodded and sighed. He didn't see any other alternative, and as much as he hated the idea, it made sense. Bri made the hotel reservations, and Obie humphed and paced while the officers finished up.

"Son, are you really all right?" his dad asked.

"Yes and no," he answered honestly. "Harvey is desperate, there's no doubt about that. But he doesn't really know what he's doing. I think he's acting on instinct and out of pure, unadulterated hatred, but there isn't a great deal of planning involved. If he wanted to get to Bri, he could have waited until he was alone and attacked him." Not that he wanted that for a second. The thought of Bri being in danger alternately filled him with fear and then anger.

"He didn't necessarily know he was here," James explained as Bri drew closer. "My guess is that he saw the two of you together, maybe at the club, but more likely at the game." James grinned slightly. "You aren't exactly subtle. He found out who you were and made an appointment." He sighed. "We don't really know what he knows, but we'll find out." Then James turned away to talk to a few of the officers, while another approached with an iPad.

"I have something, sir," she said and brought up a picture. "Is this the man who was here?" She showed it to Obie, and he nodded.

"That's him. Did he give his real name?" That was probably the stupidest move in history.

"No. But he did provide his real address, or at least most of it. He didn't have time to completely lie on the form, so he changed a few things. He used a house number that doesn't exist, but the rest was enough to follow. He figured he was being clever, but we can get around stuff like that." She turned to James. "His real name is Harvey Hamel," she said, and Bri gasped, stepping closer.

"Can I see the picture?" he asked, and she showed it to him.

"Is he familiar to you?" she asked as Bri held the iPad, his knuckles turning white as he gripped it.

"What is it?" Obie asked, becoming concerned.

"Hamel was Willy's last name. Is he a relative?" Bri asked, and provided the details he could remember.

"Let me check and see what I can find." The officer took the iPad, tapping it as she walked back toward her car.

"You think this could have something to do with Willy?" Obie asked, trying to get his head around it. "But you didn't hurt him, right? You never picked on him."

"No. But I didn't help him either," Bri said.

"Give us a chance to look into this. It could be the first solid lead into a motive that we have," his dad explained, and Obie nodded.

"Come on, Bri. We need to get out of the way so they can finish up." He turned to his dad. "Can we go inside and get some clothes for tonight? Then we can get out of here, and you can do what you need to."

"Yeah. Go right on upstairs, and I'll make sure the house is locked up when we're done." He hugged Obie once again. "You gave me a real fright, son. I'm proud of the way you handled yourself, but

I don't think I can take another close call like that." He gently stroked Obie's head. "You scared me half to death."

"I didn't mean to. It wasn't like I intended to let a deranged lunatic into the house. I think I need to add that question to the intake form." He smiled, trying to lighten the mood.

"I'm being serious. I was frightened," his dad said, and Obie closed his eyes, hugging his father back.

"I knew you'd be here. I heard him on the phone to Bri and knew in my heart that he'd call you and you'd get here faster than anyone. When I startled him, I figured I was going to buy some time, but I got away and…." He took a deep breath, letting his father comfort him. It had been some time since his dad had done that.

"Still, I…." His dad sighed. "I know I can't keep you locked away so you'd always be safe, but sometimes I wish I could." Obie supposed that was what every father wished they could do for their children. "You and Bri get to the hotel, and don't stop anywhere along the way unless you really have to. Call me once you're in the room, and throw all the locks to make double sure."

"We will, Dad," Obie agreed and stepped back. "And thanks for everything." He waited for Bri and let him go inside first, taking the direct route upstairs. It didn't take long to get what they needed and then they were out and into a car. While they rode, Obie called his remaining clients for the day to reschedule their appointments. The next two days were going to be very busy, but he got everything settled by the time they reached the Loews downtown.

Obie carried their bags as Bri checked them in. "We're on the concierge level, which requires an access card to get up to the floor. I thought it better." He handed Obie a card as the elevator door closed and they rode to the top floor. Their room was at the very end of the hall, and Obie slipped his card into the lock and they stepped into a huge suite. "Maybe I should have gotten you your own room, but I thought if we were together, it would be safer than each of us being alone. I can take one bedroom and you can have the other."

Bri headed for the room to the left, and Obie set down the bags. "I knew you'd take care of things."

"How did you know he called me?" Bri asked at the open doorway to his bedroom.

"I overheard him talking to you when I came to. I had tried to get away, but he tackled me and tried to knock me out." The rest of the story Bri already knew. "You saved me." He stepped closer to Bri, who didn't move.

"It looked to me like you saved yourself. It was your quick thinking that got you out of there." He set his crutches against the wall as Obie closed the distance between them. "I was frantic as soon as I got that call. I swear the phone shook the entire time I was talking to your dad. I told the driver to go right over to your house, and then you flew outside." Bri held him tightly, nearly crushing Obie in the fierceness of the embrace. "I don't think I was ever so happy to see anyone in my life." He slanted his lips over Obie's, kissing him gently at first, but in a fraction of a second, it went from comfort to craving.

He pressed himself to Bri, holding him fiercely, returning the kiss. "I was scared, but things I'd been told since I was a kid came back to me and they worked. All I could think of was you and that you were safe."

"Do you still want to take things slow and—?" Bri didn't get the words out. Obie cut them off with his lips, sliding his hands under Bri's shirt, caressing his taut, smooth skin over rippled muscle that sent a surge of passion racing through him.

"I...." Obie buried his face in Bri's neck, holding him as the weight of what happened settled on him. "I could have died," he whispered, half in shock at how fast everything in his head had changed.

Bri slowly guided them toward the bed and helped Obie down. His hands shook as the realization of what could have happened washed over him. Bri lay next to him, holding him tightly.

"It's all right to be scared," Bri whispered.

"But when it was happening, I was so clearheaded. And now, I can barely think straight," Obie said, not really understanding what was going on.

Bri rubbed his back and hummed slowly. "It's like that in stressful situations. I get that way after a game. I can think clearly during it, but afterward, I sort of come down and wonder what would have happened if I'd done something differently. That's what's happening here. You were cool under pressure. That's what really matters." Obie lifted his head and Bri nodded. "Most people can't do that. They freeze or panic. You did neither and you got away."

Obie took a deep breath, snuggling closer to Bri's heat and comfort. "I never want to go through that again." His phone rang, and Obie answered it. "I'm fine, Dad. We're in the hotel room."

"Good. We're working to find this guy. We checked his house, but he hasn't come back. There are signs that he packed some things, so…." His dad's voice held anger and frustration just under the surface.

"We're safe and on the concierge level, so it has additional precautions about who can get up here." He explained which hotel they were at and gave his dad the room number. "I think Bri and I are going to get something to eat. There's a nice restaurant here, so we'll get some food and wait things out until you get this guy."

"Good idea. I'll call as soon as I have anything." His dad paused. "I love you." Obie had no doubt that his dad loved him, but he wasn't one to say the words often. Hearing them meant a lot.

"Love you too," he said and ended the call, putting his phone on the nightstand and lying back down. Bri continued rubbing his back, and as the tension eased, Obie dozed off for a while.

Bri was on the phone to his parents when Obie woke, his stomach rumbling loudly. "Why don't you get up and we'll go down for something to eat? You'll feel better, and then we can watch some movies or something." He was so kind, and Obie nodded, leaning closer, pulling some calm strength from Bri. "I'm so glad you're okay. I…." Bri huffed. "I'm absolute crap when it comes to telling people how I feel. It's hard, and I'm always afraid—but I want this to work between us. I want you and me to have a chance. I knew that for sure the moment I got that call. It was like something clicked in my head. I swear if I'd had a car, I would have figured out a way for

162

the damned thing to sprout wings on the way there." Bri gathered him into his arms and held him, rocking slowly. It was amazing to be held and comforted, cherished even.

"You're good at this." Obie was surprisingly content and didn't want to move. His belly growled again, though, and he slowly got up off the bed, looking around for his shoes.

"I put them over by the door," Bri said, and Obie nodded and went over to get them. "I also checked and found out that they have a gym on the fifth floor. It has a sauna and steam room. I thought after dinner, we could relax a little, and maybe we can have a therapy session there. Get my leg working again." Bri rubbed his knee around the brace. "I really want to get rid of this thing."

"Sounds like a plan," Obie agreed and waited in the living area while Bri used the bathroom. When he joined him without the crutches, Obie didn't say anything, and they walked slowly down the hallway. He called for the elevator, and they stepped inside, riding downward quickly.

The black, marble-walled lobby was a hub of activity. "Can I help you gentlemen?" a hotel employee asked as they approached the sports bar area.

"Is the restaurant open?" Obie asked, eyeing the quieter area beyond.

"Yes. Let me show you to a table." She led them through to a much more evening-themed area that was quieter and more gently lit. They sat down in the comfortable chairs, and their server approached, taking drink orders and handing them menus.

Obie sat back, watching Bri as he mused over the menu. It was a little expensive, and Obie wondered if they should just go to the sports bar for a burger. "I want the New York strip," Bri said. "I need some steak. They have great salads and a few portobello dishes. Just get whatever you want." He seemed happy, and Obie settled on a nice salad and portobello mushroom lasagna. They gave the server their orders, and she brought bread.

"We have the entire place to ourselves," Bri said quietly. "I like that."

"Do you go out often?" Obie asked, as a man and boy walked through the restaurant.

"Mr. Early," the boy said, and Bri pasted on a smile, turning as they approached. "Can I have your autograph?" He must have been seven, and Bri signed the paper for him. "Thank you." He gave Bri a missing-front-teeth smile, clutching the paper.

"We saw you at the charity game," the father said, beaming at Bri. The kid pointed at Obie, whispering to his dad.

"He was there too. He won the ball." The boy practically bounced on his heels.

"I tried to get one of the balls for him, but wasn't able to make the shot."

"Obie and I will be here for a while. If you want to get a ball, I'd be happy to sign it for you. Just don't tell anyone." Bri winked, and the boy jumped, pulling his dad out toward the front door. Apparently, they were going shopping.

"That was very nice of you," Obie said.

"I would have given them a ball if I'd had one. I usually keep a couple in my trunk, just in case."

Obie shook his head. "I know it's not what most guys do, but being nice to your fans is a small price to pay."

"Yes, it is." He couldn't help smiling.

"Mr. Early," the boy called from across the room ten minutes later, running toward their table with a ball in his hands, still in the box. "Will you really sign it?"

"Of course," Bri said. "What's your name?"

"Zack," he answered exuberantly, and Obie hid his smile behind his water glass.

Bri signaled the server and asked if they had a Sharpie or something permanent. She returned with a thick-tipped black pen, and Bri inscribed the ball, signing and dating it for him. "There you go. I hope you enjoy it." Bri handed back the ball and shook Zack's hand. "You take good care of your dad, okay?" He nodded and hurried to where his father waited nearby, showing it to him and half skipping back toward the lobby.

Obie couldn't help chuckling softly to himself, watching him go. The server's black pants and shirt passed in front of his gaze, and then she placed his salad in front of him. It looked amazing, and Obie inhaled before picking up his fork. The mixed greens and poached pear made his mouth water and his stomach rumble. Obie probably ate faster than he should have if he wanted to savor the tanginess, but he was too hungry to eat more slowly. "Man, this is good," Obie groaned as he sat back. The server appeared, took his plate, and set down his lasagna and Bri's entree.

It smelled heavenly, and Bri cut into his huge steak, humming his happiness as he ate. "They really know how to cook here." Bri ate quickly, their conversation falling off as they both sated their hunger. When the time came, they declined dessert, and Bri charged the meal to the room. "There's a sundry shop just around the corner off the lobby. Did you want to grab some snacks for later?"

"I'll go see what they have." Obie got up and left the table, striding through the lobby and around to the shop. He got some soft drinks, chocolate, and some other candy and nuts, paying and grabbing the bag. When he left the shop, he turned the corner to the elevator bay and saw Bri waiting for him. Only he wasn't waiting.

As Obie watched, Bri stumbled slightly into the elevator—with Harvey's hand on his back. Obie raced over, but the doors slid closed before he could get there. His heart sank and he swore under his breath, wondering what in the hell to do next. Taking a deep breath, he forced himself to think.

Obie watched the display as the car rose, and pulled out his phone. "Dad, Harvey is here at the hotel and he just forced Bri into an elevator. They stopped at the twelfth floor according to the elevator readout, but I have no idea what room they're in." His legs shook as he began pacing.

"I'll get people right over there. Stay in the lobby and wait for us. Do not try to go after him. Hang on." The line went quiet and Obie waited a minute before his dad returned to the line. "I have people on their way. Just stay there."

"But—"

"Obie, you could get hurt. Please just stay where you are and let us handle it."

"Okay," he agreed reluctantly, worried about Bri and what this madman would do to him.

CHAPTER 11

BRI GOT off the elevator on the twenty-fourth floor. Harvey had practically yanked him out of the first elevator and pushed him into another one, a knife pressed to his side. "I'm going to make sure you get what you deserve."

Bri nearly stumbled as Harvey shoved him up to a door. He stood still, the point of the knife at his side dugging in with enough force to hurt, as Harvey opened the room and threw him inside. Bri managed to fall onto the bed without hurting his knee, but how, he didn't know. "Why are you doing this?"

"Why?" The door banged shut. "You nearly killed my brother and you're asking me why?" He stalked over to Bri, leaning over him, knife at the ready. He really thought he was going to die any second.

"I never hurt Willy. He and I used to sit up together sometimes and talk. But I never did anything to him. Your brother was a good man and I liked him." Harvey's eyes darkened and his hand shook in what Bri thought was rage. Bri figured logic and the truth weren't going to get him anywhere. "What happened to him after he left school?"

"Of course you don't know, Mr. Big Shot Basketball Player. He wasn't important enough for you to find out." Harvey yanked over the desk chair and sat where he could watch Bri, playing with the knife in his shaking hand. "After you all put that lavender shit in his room, he went into allergic shock and nearly died. You all thought it was funny. Willy came out of it, but his lungs were permanently damaged. He needed oxygen and help breathing for over a decade until he died, painfully." He swiped the knife forward, and Bri jumped back. Harvey grinned evilly. "I admired you. But then this happened with Willy. I knew you were involved, but no, the golden boy got off and they found someone else to pin it on. They even got the guy to

167

confess. No one was going to let the golden boy take the fall, not even one who might have been light in the loafers."

A knock sounded on the door. "Security." The voice sounded off, but Bri breathed a sigh of relief.

"You make a sound and I will gut you like a pig," Harvey growled.

"We're fine, come back later," Harvey called through the door. There was no answer, and Bri's spirit plummeted.

Another knock. "Sorry, can't do that. We need to come in. There's been a disturbance reported." This time, Bri recognized the voice. What the hell, and how did Obie find him and get up here?

"You," Harvey said, pointing the knife at Bri in a warning, "don't move." Then Harvey went to the door and opened it a crack. "I'm not decent. Can you come back—"

Harvey flew back as the door slammed open, Obie propelling himself inside the room. The knife dropped to the floor, and Bri caught a glint as it sailed along the carpet. Obie stood over Harvey, yanking him down and onto his stomach, digging his knee into Harvey's back as he pulled his arms behind him.

"That hurts," Harvey groaned.

"Then you should think before you hold people I love at knifepoint." Obie held still. "Bri, my phone is in my pocket."

Bri hesitated, parsing what Oboe had just said. He grinned, letting the words sink in before fishing out Obie's phone. Bri needed to do what he'd been asked to, but damned if he didn't smile doing it. "I'll call your dad." He pressed the contact and the phone rang once. "James, it's Bri. We have him. Room 2415. Hurry."

"Son of a bitch. He didn't wait, did he?" James swore. Bri turned to Obie, flashing him a smile.

"You should know him better than that. He's fucking fearless." And Obie had just said he loved him. Bri found it hard to breathe as he thought about it. "Just get here before he smears Harvey all over this carpet." His only concern, now that his heart rate had slowed to something a little closer to normal, was that Obie was okay.

"Let me up. So, help me, I'll sue you for everything you have."

"Bullshit. You move, and I'll break your back. So stay still. The police are on their way and they'll take care of you." Obie leaned a little closer. "You picked on the wrong guys, idiot." Officers raced closer, their boots thumping in the hall, belts clinking.

"Freeze," the officers called.

"It's okay, guys," Bri explained. "That's Obie, the commissioner's son. He got here first. The guy on the floor is the one you want. His knife is over here. No one but him has touched it." Bri stayed back as James raced in as well. The officers took Harvey into custody, and the questions began from James, aimed at Obie with all the force of a hurricane.

"I'm fine, Dad," Obie said, but his father didn't look mollified in the least.

"How did you know where to find them?" James finally asked, his ears turning red with what Bri thought was growing anger.

Obie shrugged as though it were easy. "I simply explained to the woman at the front desk that my boyfriend had been kidnapped and the police were on their way. I described the man who had done it, and the lady said he had checked in an hour before. I may have used your name a little, and she got flustered and gave me the room number. I just pretended to be security that wouldn't go away. When he opened it a crack, I kicked the door in and laid him on his ass. It was all pretty simple. I'm a policeman's kid. You made sure I knew how to protect myself, Dad. And I did," Obie explained as though it was nothing. Then he left the room and returned with a white plastic bag, handing it to Bri.

"Of course you brought the snacks," Bri teased, holding it up and rolling his eyes. He set it back down on the bed. "Why don't we let your dad and the police ask their questions so we can go home?" Two attempted kidnappings in the same day had his nerves on edge. As nice as this hotel was, he didn't want to stay here any longer than he had to.

"That sounds like a plan to me," James said and stepped back so the officers could do their job. They ended up back in their suite, where Bri got comfortable and explained what had happened.

"He appeared behind me. All I can figure out is that he followed us." Bri sat back on the sofa, looking around the empty room. Obie always filled a space with life and warmth, and he'd come close to losing him. Hell, twice in a way, and it sent a chill through him that wouldn't go away. Bri glanced toward the door again and then back at the officer as he answered question after question. Finally, the key clicked in the lock and Obie came inside, looking a little worse for wear. He came over and sat right next to Bri, winding his arm around his.

"Did he say why he'd done all this?" James asked as he followed Obie inside.

"He was Willy's brother and he blamed me for what happened. Apparently, the stunt his roommate pulled damaged Willy's lungs permanently."

"Yes. It seems William Hamel passed away about six months ago. And that probably pushed his brother over the edge. He truly believes that you were the cause of his brother's death. I requested a copy of the case file, and it was emailed over. The roommate admitted responsibility in the end, and did some time for what happened. The record shows that you weren't involved, but I somehow doubt that in his state of mind, Harvey would be swayed by something as inconsequential as the facts." James sat in one of the chairs across from them. "Do you have everything you need?' James asked the officer who'd been questioning Bri.

"Yes, thanks. I'll leave the three of you." He got up and left the room, presumably returning to join the others.

"What now, Dad?" Obie said.

"Well, we have him pretty much dead to rights, but…." He slowly shook his head. "From here, we'll have to let the courts decide. As for the two of you, you can stay in the hotel or go back home. We finished at the house and can connect him to what happened there. It's up to you." James leaned forward, a glare in his eyes that made Bri squirm. "It's probably a bad time to mention it, but I assume you know what I'll do if you hurt him." James held his gaze.

"Dad, stop it." Obie leaned closer, resting against Bri's arm. "I really just want to go home." He buried his face against Bri's shoulder, and Bri held Obie's hand a little tighter.

"Then I'll call down and tell them that we're checking out." Bri spoke softly, but he'd do whatever Obie wanted. He didn't move, scooting even closer and holding Bri a little tighter. Bri turned slightly, holding Obie in return. Bri barely registered that James had left the room, and they sat together in silence, holding one another.

"I never want to have a day like this again," Obie muttered. "I was so scared. Dad told me to just wait in the lobby." Obie lifted his face away, and Bri knew it was unlikely that Obie would ever do what he was told. Thank God. He had his own mind and was going to follow it.

"So was I," Bri admitted. "At first, I was afraid for you, and then he kept poking me with that knife." He took a deep breath and tried not to think about what could have happened and what he could have lost. "This whole ordeal has been way too much." He never wanted to go through anything like that again.

Bri didn't want to move. He was content and needed Obie in his arms. "I'm sorry I was so stupid," Obie whispered. Bri wondered where that came from and turned to look at him. Obie's gaze met his and then their lips met and Obie shifted, pressing harder against him.

Bri found it hard to breathe or think. Obie climbed onto his knees without breaking the kiss, pressing him down onto the cushions. He was starting to get a pretty good idea of what Obie thought he was sorry for. "Hey," he said, holding Obie's cheeks in his hands. "You've been through a lot in the last four hours. Are you sure about this?"

Obie paused, and Bri slowly sat back up. "We've both been running on adrenaline for hours, and…."

"Bri, I'm sure. I think this whole ethics thing was a way of keeping my distance because I've been scared. My relationships don't usually work out, and you're a famous basketball player. I kept wondering what you could possibly see in me. So I… I don't know. I think I came up with this whole client/therapist thing to keep from getting hurt. I kept figuring you'd wake up any minute and run

screaming from the house, but all I ever saw was just the opposite."
He sighed and hugged him, resting his head on Bri's shoulder. "I just
want to go home, I think, and then maybe you and I can talk and
watch some television while I have a complete panic attack over how
I took on a knife-wielding kidnapper all by myself and probably could
have gotten us both killed."

Yeah, Bri had made the right decision for now. All this excitement
and adrenaline was going to take a toll on both of them. Neither of
them needed to do something they'd regret. Besides, when he made
love to Obie, he wanted it to be under more romantic, less desperate
circumstances. "Okay. Let's get our things and we can explain what
happened. I'm sure the hotel will take care of things." They probably
would have if either of them had moved to ask. Instead, they sat
silently together, holding each other for almost an hour.

"Did you mean what you said?" Bri whispered after a while.
"Do you really love me?"

"Yeah." Obie turned to him, swallowing, his throat working,
and Bri knew he was anxious. "Ummm."

"Sweetheart, I love you too."

"So you don't mind waiting until we can get you back on your
feet and…." Obie bit his lower lip.

Bri nodded. "I'll wait for you as long as you need me to." He
closed the distance between them, holding Obie even closer. Sex was
one thing, but love, being loved, that was worth any wait.

CHAPTER 12

FOR DAYS, Obie was barely out of Bri's sight. They both seemed to need to have the other one close. The two of them slept together, but nothing else had happened. Obie had finished up his morning appointments in his fully cleaned and newly sanitized therapy room. He'd had to wipe down everything Harvey might have touched in order to fully eradicate him from his workspace. With nothing to do, he paced the room, waiting for Bri to get back from the doctor.

He thought about doing some more cleaning, but figured he was getting a little obsessive. Obie had already been through the entire house, just in case Harvey had been in there, and cleaned everything to within an inch of its life. No dust bunny was safe from this jag.

"What did the doctor say?" Obie asked as he hurried toward the back door when it opened. Bri had replaced his car and no longer needed to use Uber to get around. Obie skidded to a stop as Bri came into the kitchen without his brace. "Good news, I guess."

"Yes." Bri leaned down and kissed him. "I don't need the brace any longer, and he said that my knee had healed remarkably well. I have more movement in it than he ever expected." His smile lit the room. "And that's all because of you."

"So what are you saying?" Obie asked.

"That I need to take it easy. But I saw the team doctor as well, and he sees no reason why I won't be able to join the team for preseason workouts. I should be ready and able to play the regular season." He engulfed Obie in a tight hug.

"So…." Obie humphed softly.

"That means that while I'll need continued exercise for strength, I should be good to go on the therapy angle." Bri nuzzled the base of Obie's neck, and he groaned. "So, officially, I'm no longer a client, which means that you—Obie Kenoble—are definitely on the

173

celebratory menu." Bri took his hand and walked steadily through the house. "I'd run, but the doc said to work up to things."

"I see," Obie said, grinning.

"Yeah, and I've been working up to that for weeks now." He climbed the stairs, and Bri led them to his bedroom, kicking the door closed as soon as Obie was inside, pressing him down onto the bed. "Let's see, no longer a client, check. No more madmen after us, check. You looking absolutely edible… check, check, check." Bri's voice deepened with every single word until it resonated down Obie's spine. He leaned over him, Bri's heat radiating through Obie's clothes. "Is there anything else standing in our way?"

Obie swallowed and shook his head. "No." Damn, all he could think of were those incredible eyes and the way they looked at him as though he was the very center of the universe. To be looked at like that, wanted that badly, was almost too much and too good to believe. But there was no mistaking it, and that was impossible to fake, as far as Obie could figure. He had to believe that this was real, and if it was, then the sexiest man he'd ever met was about to strip him bare, physically and spiritually, and make him his.

"Any other rules I should be aware of?" Bri cocked a sideways smile. "So long as I'm not breaking any rules or causing any moral dilemmas, I think I can finally—"

"Did anyone ever tell you that you talk way too damned much?" Obie groused, and pulled him down on top of him. Bri's lips found Obie's easily, his hands sliding under his shirt. Obie mewled softly under his breath as Bri found his nipples, plucking lightly and sending quivering ripples of heat running through him.

"Did anyone ever tell you that you're way too mouthy?" Bri retorted.

Obie humphed. *Did he know him at all?* "My dad, aunts, my whole family—in fact, basically everyone I've ever known at one time or other. And this surprises you?" His quip drifted off into a groan as Bri sucked the base of his neck. "What are you doing? Oh God."

"Giving you one hell of a hickey," he whispered, and Obie was about to protest, but gave up as Bri tugged up his shirt, getting it over

174

his head and off within seconds. As Bri kissed him, he worked Obie's pants open and down, with Obie kicking off his shoes and then the rest until he was naked.

This was Grade A naughty. At least he felt that way, with Bri still dressed. Obie pulled at his clothes, desperate to get at the rippling muscles he knew were under that red polo shirt and jeans. He didn't get very far, but then Bri slipped off the bed, standing near his feet, slowly tugging off his shirt. "Striptease?" Obie asked with a giggle as Bri rolled his eyes. "Just a minute and I'll see where I put my body glitter." Where this was coming from, he had no idea. Maybe it was the simple fact that he was happy, joyously happy.

"No, thanks." Bri pulled off his shirt, dropping it to the side of the bed, his muscles glistening with a light sheen of sweat. God, he was stupendously amazing, and when his shoes and then pants joined the pile, and Bri stood in front of him in all his naked glory, Obie's mouth went dry. He could only nod slowly.

"No glitter... right." Obie grinned, staring up at Bri. "Not that you need anything to get you more attention." Hell, he'd watch him forever, especially as Bri stalked closer. "Don't hurt yourself, whatever you do."

Bri nodded and turned to the side, giving a little hip thrust and then a burlesque-level hip bump that sent Obie into peals of laughter. "What? I was trying to be sexy."

He covered his mouth. "It didn't work." Obie held out his hand, and Bri took it, holding tightly as he drew Bri closer. "There's no need for you to be anything but you. No fancy moves, no stripteases, and definitely no glitter. You heat up a room just by walking into it." Obie drew him down, loving the feeling of having Bri's weight on top of him and their lips together.

Obie loved kissing. In his opinion, it was as intimate, or maybe more so, than sex itself. And Bri was an amazing kisser. Heat rose between them, and Obie was afraid he was going to come just from kissing Bri. Weeks of separation, being forced apart by his ethics, only heightened the pull between them.

"I'm sorry for...."

Bri shushed him, gently slithering down his chest, peppering a trail along the way with little nips and kisses until he reached his cock. Obie wanted to say again how much he regretted the many weeks of forced celibacy, when Bri took him between his lips, stealing his ability to make any coherent sound. Not that it really mattered right now. "You taste amazing. Did I tell you that?"

Obie mumbled something along the terms of a yes, but then his eyes crossed and his breath hitched as Bri sucked him harder and deeper. "Oh my God." He thrust his hips upward, and Bri took him hard before backing away. Obie groaned at the loss.

"It's okay," Bri soothed before kissing him hard enough to send shudders through him. "I'm not stopping. I just want you to know how I feel. You are the center of my life."

"What does that mean?"

Bri sighed. "I've decided that I'm not going to back away from us. I'm not going to make some huge announcement about my private life, but I will not hide you. I don't want a bunch of attention around my life… our life. But I will never deny you or ask you to stay in the background. When we have family team events, I want you to go with me. People may talk, but that's up to them."

Obie threw his arms around Bri's neck and held him as closely and as dearly as he had ever done with anyone, at any time in his life. "Are you sure?"

"Yes. I don't want secrets to hang over us. So I'm not going to keep any. Maybe there will be some difficulties, but we'll weather them as they come along." He sighed and held still, locking his intense gaze on Obie's. "Are you with me?"

"Without a doubt," Obie answered. "That what I love about you, Bri. You make up your mind and go for it. No holds barred. It's what makes you such a good player on the court." He tugged him down into a kiss, and Bri spent the next half hour showing him just the kind of player he was in the bedroom. When Bri rolled on a condom and slid into him, Obie was over the moon in ecstasy, holding Bri as tightly as he dared, their bodies moving together, spirits joining.

Obie barely held it together as Bri slowly rocked back and forth, filling him, pushing him higher and higher. "I could spend hours talking about the things I love about you," Bri whispered, pressing deep and hard.

Obie gasped, mouth open. "Yeah…. Oh *yeah*!" He quivered as Bri pulled out, then slid back inside him, both of them groaning in wonderment.

"Yes." Bri gritted his teeth as Obie teetered on the edge. Bri had brought him here before, holding him there and then pulling him back enough times that Obie gasped. This time Bri pushed him over, his body tingling, his mind bathed in light and excitement as he plunged into a pool of passion he never wanted to climb out of.

"Oh God. Is it bad to say that this was worth waiting for?" Obie muttered half under his breath as Bri lay on the bed beside him.

"No, sweetheart," Bri whispered, lightly stroking his cheek. "But let's not wait so long before we do it again."

Obie chuckled, slowly rolling onto his side. "Okay." He leaned closer. "I love you, you know."

Bri nodded. "I do. And I love you." He pulled Obie closer. "And I have to thank you for all the assists, with my knee, at the hotel… with my life. Just by being yourself, you made me see I could do the same."

"You're welcome," Obie whispered and pulled Bri down for a kiss.

EPILOGUE

"GO GET him!" Obie yelled as Bri raced down the court. He was on his feet, much as he'd been for most of the game. "Make him pay!" He turned to his dad, who sat next to him, rolling his eyes. Obie sat down slowly. "Sorry." This was Bri's first game since he'd been injured. But it didn't look like his knee was slowing him down any.

James had given up a while ago trying to get Obie to sit down and not yell at the top of his lungs. "It's okay." He shook his head, chuckling, and then jumped to his feet along with Obie as Bri scored a basket. They sat back down again. "When I agreed to take the night off and come with you, I thought it was going to be a night off. If my days were like this at work, I'd ask for hazard pay." He rubbed his ears and his shoulder, and it was Obie's turn to roll his eyes.

This was the first game of the season, and it had been a nail-biter from the first tip-off. Needless to say, Obie had been anxious and excited from the beginning. New York was playing well. They'd replaced Young, who had been suspended indefinitely on a number of charges and was facing plenty of separate legal issues. "I'll sit down and try to be still."

New York scored, and Obie groaned as the Rockets took possession. Obie found that no matter how much the players moved around and changed positions, he always knew exactly where Bri was and watched his every move. "Forget it," his dad teased. "Just be yourself. It's good to see you happy." James put an arm around Obie's shoulder for a fatherly squeeze just as Bri hit a three-pointer. Obie shot to his feet and nearly knocked his dad out of his seat. "I'm definitely right about the hazard pay." The buzzer sounded to mark the first half, with Philadelphia up by two points.

Obie sat back down, breathing heavily and wondering if he was going to have enough nerve and energy to make it through this.

"Hey," the man behind him said, tapping him on the shoulder. Obie tensed and turned around.

"Can I help you?" Obie asked.

"It would be nice if you could stay seated. We can't see when you stand." He was a few years older than him, sneering as he spoke.

"I'll try," Obie said as his father snickered next to him. "What?" He glared at his dad.

"I somehow doubt that's possible," he said loud enough for the guy to hear him. "Really, you need to try to settle down. If you're going to come to all the games, you're going to spend a lot of time on your feet if you carry on every time Bri makes a basket."

"I noticed you have a thing for him." His voice lightened a little. "Is it the whole gay, coming out thing?" the guy asked, looking Obie over as though he was assessing him. The woman with him turned away, obviously embarrassed as hell.

"Not really." Obie stood, putting his hands on his hips. "It's more the 'I sleep with him' thing." He lifted his eyebrows and waited, challenging the man to say something derogatory.

He stammered and it was pretty clear that he wanted to die. His wife, on the other hand, began laughing. "I told you, Stan, that I recognized him." She leaned forward. "I love your hair. I tried for that color once and it was a disaster."

"I was born with it." He chuckled and turned around to sit back down. Bri jogged out onto the court, moving to where they sat in the front row. Everyone around them got to their feet and tried to get Bri's attention, but he came right over to Obie, earning him plenty of dirty looks.

"How is the knee?" Obie asked.

"It's doing okay. Probably going to be a little sore," Bri told him, "but I'm not in any pain."

Obie smiled. He wanted to kiss him, but this wasn't the place. "I'll massage it when we get home."

"James, are you enjoying the game?" Bri asked his dad.

"Yes. Though your biggest and loudest fan tends to be a little hazardous for the people around him." His dad glanced at him, teasing.

"Yes. He's a little loud." Bri smiled and turned back to Obie. "There was a message on my phone when I got back to the locker room. I've accepted an offer on my house. We'll settle in six weeks."

Obie jumped to his feet, hugging Bri. "That's great." Then he sat back down, feeling a little sheepish.

"What's even better is that the Realtor also said that the house we were looking at, the one near the park, is going to be coming up for sale. He's going to arrange for us to get an early look at it." He took Obie's hand right there in the arena. "I'll talk to you after the game and we can make plans." Bri trotted away, waving at the fans up in the seats as he took his place on the bench, the other players joining him.

Obie sat back, smiling. After the fire, Bri had decided to sell his house, and he'd moved in with Obie, full-time, a few weeks ago. Their plan was to buy a house together, and Obie had always had his eye on the neoclassical house near the park. He had no idea if it was going to be what they needed, but he really wanted to see it. He barely noticed anything until the buzzer sounded, and then his attention was back on the game.

THERE WAS less than thirty seconds to go, with Philadelphia behind by one. Unfortunately, New York had possession. They passed it in bounds and dribbled to about midcourt. The player faked left but Bri was ready for him. He snatched the ball, racing back toward the basket, the clock ticking down. *Ten, nine....* He jumped and took a shot. *Eight, seven....* Obie was on his feet, as was the rest of the stadium. *Six, five....* The ball flew through the air. *Four, three....* It hooked the rim, slid around the edge, and fell through. The buzzer sounded and everyone went absolutely wild. The cheers shook the entire arena, and Obie whistled and stomped as Bri jumped into the air along with the rest of the team.

The coach hurried over, patting Bri on the back and pressing the ball into his hands. He held it up, and the cheers began all over again. Obie grinned, his chest warming.

"That was amazing!" Obie's dad said from next to him, but Obie barely heard it. His full attention was on Bri as the team lined up to shake hands with the opposing players, who then filed off the court. Bri jogged in his direction once again, leaning over the rail, pressing the ball into Obie's hands. "None of this would have been possible without you." He leaned closer, pulled Obie to his feet, and kissed him right there. "You gave me a second chance and helped me get the rebound of a lifetime."

ANDREW GREY is the author of more than 100 works of Contemporary Gay Romantic fiction. After twenty-seven years in corporate America, he has now settled down in Central Pennsylvania with his husband, Dominic, and his laptop. An interesting ménage. Andrew grew up in western Michigan with a father who loved to tell stories and a mother who loved to read them. Since then he has lived throughout the country and traveled throughout the world. He is a recipient of the RWA Centennial Award, has a master's degree from the University of Wisconsin-Milwaukee, and now writes full-time. Andrew's hobbies include collecting antiques, gardening, and leaving his dirty dishes anywhere but in the sink (particularly when writing). He considers himself blessed with an accepting family, fantastic friends, and the world's most supportive and loving partner. Andrew currently lives in beautiful, historic Carlisle, Pennsylvania.

Email: andrewgrey@comcast.net
Website: www.andrewgreybooks.com

ALL FOR YOU

ANDREW GREY

The only path to happiness is freedom: the freedom to live—and love—as the heart wants. Claiming that freedom will take all the courage one young man has… but he won't have to face it alone.

In small, conservative Sierra Pines, California, Reverend Gabriel is the law. His son, Willy, follows his dictates… until he meets a man in Sacramento, and then reunites with him in his hometown—right under his father's nose.

Reggie is Sierra Pines's newly appointed sheriff. His dedication to the job means not announcing his sexuality, but when he sees Willy again, he can't escape the feeling that they're meant to be together. He'll keep Willy's secret until Willy is ready to let the world see who he really is. But if going up against the church and the townspeople isn't enough, the perils of the work Reggie loves so much might mean the end of their romance before it even gets off the ground….

www.dreamspinnerpress.com

NEW TRICKS

Andrew Grey

In matters of the heart, there's no such thing as business as usual.

Thomas Stepford spent years building a very successful business and now at thirty-nine, he wants a quieter life. With his parents needing help, he decides to return home. He can't get away from business completely and needs an assistant—but the man who is hired isn't quite what he had in mind.

Brandon Wilson, the ink on his degree barely dry, needs a job, and his mother helps him get one as Mr. Stepford's assistant. Thomas doesn't seem to remember, but Brandon worked mowing the stunningly attractive older man's lawn years ago. Thomas was Brandon's teenage fantasy, and now he's Brandon's boss.

Thomas and Brandon are both determined to keep their relationship strictly business, but the old attraction is still there. They learn to work together even as the tension between them reaches the boiling point. But just as they start to surrender, Thomas's old life in New York calls him. Even if he resists that pull, can their newfound relationship survive when Brandon receives the call of his dreams… from Hollywood?

www.dreamspinnerpress.com

UNFAMILIAR
WATERS

ANDREW GREY

With the pressures of the job bearing down on him, police officer Garrett Wreckley needs a vacation—in fact, he isn't given a choice in the matter. Since the water has always soothed Garrett's soul, he heads to the Caribbean, hoping some time alone sailing on the open water will help him pull himself together.

But even though he's taking a break from law enforcement, Garrett can't get rid of his cop's instinct so easily.

He meets Nigel, a young man as innocent as he is beautiful, who grew up sheltered from the world, exploring the beaches and tropical forests with only the company of his aunt, his brother, and the wildlife and sea creatures he befriended.

As sweet, passionate love blooms, their time in paradise feels too good to be true… and Garrett's gut and training tell him that might be the case. As he investigates, he quickly realizes everything is not as it seems. Will his snooping destroy not only their romance, but everything Nigel believes about his life?

www.dreamspinnerpress.com